THE MYSTERY OF RUBY'S SMOKE

ROSE DONOVAN

MORE RUBY DOVE MYSTERIES

Sign up for updates and bonus material from Ruby and Fina. Details can be found at the end of *The Mystery of Ruby's Smoke*.

Cast of Characters at Quenby College

Ruby Dove – Student of chemistry at Oxford, fashion designer and amateur spy-sleuth.

Fina Aubrey-Havelock – Student of history at Oxford, assistant seamstress to Ruby and her best friend.

Wendell Dove – Ruby's brother. A walking encyclopaedia with an unexpected profession.

Gayatri Badarur – Student of medicine at Oxford. Determined to succeed.

Pixley Hayford – Wendell's friend. A journalist eager for a scoop.

Harold Baden Gasthorpe – Popular hawker of second-rate political ideas. A journalist and lover of fame and tobacco.

Beatrice Truelove – New scout at Quenby and a fierce cleanser of dirt. Truelove by nature.

Primrose Ossington – Dean of Quenby. Defending her college from insolvency.

Esmond Bathurst – Chemistry professor with film-star good looks. And knows it, too.

Grace Yingxia – Visiting fellow and poet at Quenby. Up for an adventure.

Victoria Marlston – Professor of History who believes in rules.

Jack Devenish – Personal secretary to Gasthorpe with a misty past. Loud by nature, loud by clothing.

James Matua – First-year history student from New Zealand.

Enid Wiverton – Quenby student struggling to be herself.

Vera Sapperton – Vera the Viper. Student of chemistry with an ample budget for fashion.

Chief Inspector Hogston – Determined to find the murderer. And keep his hat on.

Detective Sergeant Snorscomb – Whistling sidekick to Hogston.

Constable Clumber – Caped constable on the case.

Tiberius (Tibby) – The college cat. Like his namesake, a tyrannical recluse.

1

A glowing globe of embers turned orange and scarlet.

"Lies, lies, a tissue of lies!" exclaimed Fina, stamping her foot. She crumpled up another sheet of newspaper and hurled it into the grate. The flames lapped at the paper.

Letting out a screech of frustration, she stamped her other foot. "And another thing. If this Harold Baden what's-his-face—"

"Gasthorpe," supplied Ruby helpfully.

"Yes, this Mr Gasbag as he shall be known henceforth," said Fina, with a grand, sweeping gesture that nearly dislodged Ruby's beret from her head. "If he thinks he will get away with this travesty, he is sadly misinformed." Fina plopped down in the nearest chair and blew a puff of air at her fringe. She slumped down further into the armchair, arms akimbo.

Though Ruby had politely put aside her sketch of a rather marvellous mauve gown while Fina unleashed her tirade, she took up her pad again. Fina knew she was waiting for her to calm down.

"I'm finished. Tirade over. Sorry, but not sorry," said Fina with a grin at her friend. Fina reflected on their past year or so at Oxford. They had become close enough to know what would make each of them as bitter as bile. The friendship had survived two murder investigations, the first in a snowed-in manor in England, the second on a cruise in the Caribbean. Not to mention their political escapades, which, if they hadn't been careful, could have landed them in very hot water indeed.

"So, this Gasthorpe," began Ruby, deftly drawing a pillbox hat on the next sketch page.

"Please, we must call him Mr Gasbag."

The corner of Ruby's mouth lifted in amusement. "I've heard of him, of course. He wrote that book that is attracting enormous attention. Something about an English trip?"

Fina giggled and rolled her eyes. She said in her best faux-upper-class accent, "*English Passage*, duckie. *All* the rage."

"Good Lord," said Ruby, not looking up from the evening cape on her sketchpad. "I could tell you a few things about English passages."

"Yes, well, it's this blasted book. It's made him famous. He's now the darling of the Labour party, suffragettes, and the left in general."

"So why all the fuss?"

"Because..." said Fina, sucking in a great gulp of air, "he calls Irish people savages. And says Irish independence proves we're an ungovernable, uncivilised people. And I won't even tell you what he said about the colonies. I'm sure you can imagine it."

Ruby nodded as if this were expected. But Fina noticed Ruby's jaw clench and her hand tighten around her fountain pen.

"So that's what makes him so dangerous in particular – because he's on the left," said Fina softly.

Ruby set aside her pad again. "But what is it that has made you so incensed?"

Fina stared at the fireplace. The flames had consumed the little balls of paper. Rain pattered on the windows of her small but eminently cosy room at college. She was proud of the way she had made it her own, with a cherry-red counterpane on her rather narrow bed, a small tea station in the corner, and plenty of pillows scattered around the room for comfort. Her mantel held a bowl with a sweet-smelling mixture of lavender, rose hips, and orange peel. She had strung a delicate line of fairy lights in early anticipation of the holidays. Even though it was only October.

She glanced at the photograph of her family on the mantel, almost subconsciously. It was the only photo she had of her mother, father, and brother, Connor. It was right at the end of the ledge, facing the door, and a casual observer might have thought its location meant she was estranged from her family. If they only knew.

Ruby sat still, as if she were waiting for Fina to process something terribly important.

Fina cleared her throat and held on to the arms of her chair for dear life. "Not only is he a colonial lackey of the worst sort, but he used my family, as an example..." She trailed off as her lips began to tremble.

Reaching over to pat her on the knee, Ruby said quietly, "It's about your brother and father, isn't it?"

"Yes." The tears began to roll down Fina's cheeks, though her face remained impassive. "He said the way my brother killed my father is an example of how Irish depravity is inborn – because my mother is Irish and my father was English. Then he had the audacity to compare it to the way Ireland has reacted to England – biting the hand that feeds you and all that rot."

"I'm so sorry, Feens." Ruby paused. "I know how painful this is for you. You know he's spouting off with the hope of gaining attention. Like an irritable child who finds out he's not the centre of the universe after all."

Fina wiped away her tears and nodded. "It's so beastly to

have these incessant reminders. At first I wanted to know more but now I want to put it behind me."

Ruby stood up and began to pace in front of the fireplace. Fina knew what that meant. Something was bothering her.

"What's wrong? Are you worried about the newspaper coverage?"

First Ruby nodded, but then shook her head. "Of course I'm worried about that for your sake. But I've been avoiding telling you my news."

2

Fina gulped and gripped the arms of her chair again, bracing for impact.

Gliding toward her chair, Ruby rummaged around in her bag until she found her quarry. A postcard. She handed it over to Fina without a word.

The picture postcard had a bucolic scene of St George's in Grenada on the front. Flipping it over, Fina saw it was from Ian Clavering, Ruby's ... who was Ian to Ruby? Perhaps he was her muse. They had met Ian on their first mission and mystery, at Pauncefort Hall. And then again at sea. She knew Ruby was inexorably attracted to Ian, but didn't trust him. He popped up at the most opportune times, certainly.

"Are you sure you want me to read this? Isn't it personal?" asked Fina.

Ruby gave her head a vigorous shake. Methinks the lady doth protest too much, thought Fina. Ruby's eyes were narrowed, though. There must be more to it than her hot-cold feelings toward Ian.

The postcard was addressed to Ruby at her address in Quenby College:

August 1935.

Dear Ruby,

Greetings from Grenada. I'm here to visit my aunt and to spend a few days on the beach – though you know I'm having trouble relaxing. Especially without you. Hope to hear from you soon.

Yours,
Ian

Fina looked up at Ruby. "Am I missing something? It seems like a mundane – if a little insipid – postcard. Is that why you wanted me to see it?"

"No. I wondered if you noticed anything odd about it."

Fina scrutinised the card, handwriting and words. She was concentrating so intently she noticed her mouth was hanging open. Snapping it shut, she handed the card back to Ruby.

"I'm stumped."

"Observe the stamp," said Ruby, holding up the card as if she were one of their lecturers. "It's upside down. That's a signal. A signal something is wrong, very wrong. It means danger."

An antique clock on the mantel sounded once. The noise nearly made Fina jump out of her seat. It was as if she had never heard a clock chiming.

Ruby looked down at her tiny wristwatch. "Come, I'll be late for my chemistry lecture."

"But what about your news? You can't tell me Ian sent you a warning and then not tell me more!"

"Of course," said Ruby as she began to pack up her small bag. "You don't have class until later, so why don't you join me? I cannot miss the first day of class. Besides, the new chemistry don is quite dishy. Let's hurry or I'll be late!"

Fina sprang into action, first patting down her hair – as if that would do anything to tame it. Then she scooped up her green bouclé woollen coat and soft burgundy leather bag. It was a present from her mother for the beginning of the new term.

Spinning around once on her heel, she checked to make sure she hadn't forgotten anything. The fire. She took the jug down from a nearby bookshelf and poured its contents over the smouldering embers. Those little balls of paper had disappeared.

Out on the quad, the clouds had parted and a golden autumn glow suffused the afternoon light, outlining their lengthening shadows. Michaelmas term was her favourite. She enjoyed the clash between the smell of decaying leaves and the anticipation of a new academic year. Students trundled like ants along the pathways of the college, nearly colliding with the occasional don lost in thought.

She smiled as she watched the college cat, Tiberius – or Tibby, as he was known by the undergraduates – slink toward a corner of the quad. Fina loved cats, but she generally steered clear of Tibby. He was the college curmudgeon, surpassing even the saltiest don. Tibby wiggled back and forth, preparing to pounce on some unwitting mouse near the wall. He shot his lean body underneath the building. There must be a hole underneath, she thought. A minute later, Tibby emerged, disappointed and covered in dust. As if to cover his embarrassment, he stood in the sunlight, casually licking his paw.

As they rounded the corner into the lecture hall, Fina almost bumped into someone with her head down. Fina caught herself by leaning against the rough red brick of the hall.

"Gayatri!" said Ruby and Fina in unison. They embraced each other like long-lost relatives.

"It's been ages," said Ruby. "I haven't seen you since Pauncefort Hall! Where have you been? Did you go home to Tezpur?"

Gayatri shook her head. "No, unfortunately not. We simply didn't have the money. It wasn't a bother because Oxford is my home – for now. Besides, I had to study. My exams are coming up soon so I decided it was best to stay in college and work as hard as I could."

"Are you at Quenby now rather than Somerville?" queried Ruby.

Gayatri pursed her lips. "I had differences of opinion with the warden of Somerville. Or rather, I should say she had some with me. So here I am – and I'm quite contented."

She squinted at Fina. "Weren't you studying at St Jude's?"

Nodding sadly, Fina said, "My absences were piling up, so I'm afraid I had a disagreement with the warden as well." She waved her hand around their surroundings. "But I find Quenby much more amenable in any case."

Ruby enquired, "How is your sister? Is she here?"

"Unfortunately, no. Sajida went home, but I do expect her back soon."

Fina surveyed Gayatri a little more closely. She wore her favourite earthy-brown tone. While she brimmed with that peculiar beginning-of-term energy, she looked rather gaunt. Gaunt in the sense of someone worried, and too busy to eat or take care of oneself. Must have been the studying during the summer. Not enough proper time to rest, she thought.

Gayatri glanced at her watch. "Are you on your way to the chemistry lecture, Ruby?" She looked at Fina and gently touched her shoulder. "I didn't mean not to include you, Fina, but I didn't think a history scholar would be joining a chemistry lecture!"

"I'm just tagging along for the ride," said Fina with a smile. "I heard about this new professor."

Gayatri laughed. "Yes, it does feel like royalty coming to

visit." Fina laughed to herself at Gayatri's utter lack of self-consciousness about being a princess herself.

With that, the three made their way up the stairs, through the imposing gothic arches and down into the bowels of Wandesford Hall.

3

The room was as packed as a crowded beehive. Students spilled out of the aisles. A few leaned against the wall, as if they were about to take a cigarette break. Others set up camp on the floor. Fina observed she wasn't the only one in the hall who wasn't a science student. She recognised James Matua, a first-year history student from New Zealand. They had struck up a conversation outside the Radcliffe Camera after he spotted her copy of Mulk Raj Anand's *Untouchable* tucked under her arm. The book had just been published and was all the rage in leftist political circles. Fina had to admit to James she hadn't read the book yet, which prompted him to launch into a long diatribe against the colonial overlords – particularly those in New Zealand. The fact that Fina listened to his discourse was enough to endear her to him. And she admired his earnestness.

Tall and lean, James lounged near the back entrance. His rather contrived aloof manner barely concealed the earnest nervousness which often infects first-year students. He raised his head to allow his hair to flip back from covering his eyes. She approved of his hunter-green suit. Clearly a new purchase – and tailor-made as well. It looked like he was trying oh-so-hard, and Fina found it rather charming.

As he turned away, she watched him with the fascination – though not the fear – of a mouse before a snake. He pulled a sheet of paper from his briefcase and laid it carefully out in front of him, ready to take notes. Then, putting down his pen, he tore the corner off the paper, being careful to keep the tear running precisely along the line of an imaginary quarter-circle. He crumpled up the torn-off piece in his hand. After looking from side to side, he popped the scrap of paper into his mouth and began to chew. As if it were chewing gum. And then he swallowed.

A pause – and the whole process began again. Another perfectly semi-circular piece of paper was torn off and munched up. Fina would have stayed to watch if she hadn't been pushed along by the crowd to find a seat.

Gayatri, Ruby and Fina found seats together, even though they were unfortunately in the front row. Fina had toyed with the idea of leaving early but clearly this was no longer going to be an option. She settled down in the hard seat, preparing for a long afternoon.

Fina turned around to survey the tittering students. The professor was late. It was an excellent way to start the first day of class – if you were a man, of course. A woman professor who was tardy would be seen as scattered and disorganised.

A pair of students behind her confirmed her own internal diatribe.

"Professor Bathurst must be late coming from an important meeting."

"Or perhaps he's had a breakthrough in the laboratory."

And. Then. He. Entered. Fina could sense Ruby and Gayatri stiffening next to her. The rustling and humming noise was turned down like the volume on a Victrola. Heart racing, Fina looked at her friends. They were transfixed. No wonder. This godlike man, clad in the traditional robes of the professoriate, was good-looking in an unconventional, craggy sort of way. But he definitely had presence. Presence that now filled the room.

He slid his small briefcase across a table. Then he deftly removed a sheaf of papers and twirled around behind the lectern. Fina felt sure he might pull out a cane and begin to dance.

"Let us begin," he said in a gravelly voice. Not like rocky gravel, but pebbles, smoothed by hundreds of years of ocean waves.

He gripped the podium and began. He talked about ancient herbal chemists and the healing power of plants. He then transitioned abruptly to the marvels of modern chemistry. Rubber. Sugar. Bauxite.

Gayatri leaned over Ruby's notebook and scribbled something in the margins. She gave Ruby a knowing glance. Then Ruby wrote in Fina's notebook. "And we all know about rubber, sugar and bauxite!"

Fina smiled at the two of them, nodding her head. Indeed, they knew all about what it took to produce these chemically altered products. All too well. The irony of her own comfort was a point not lost on Fina – but it still made her angry to think about what she knew about sugar plantations. She thought back to the horrifying letter they had discovered at Pauncefort Hall last Christmas. The injustices detailed in the letter had been rectified, but not before two murders had been committed.

Enraptured by his subject – or by the sound of his own voice – Professor Bathurst paced like a tiger in front of the podium. He periodically threw up his hands to make a particular point. And then he came to an abrupt halt. A pencil had rolled to a stop at his feet. He bent over and scooped it up.

"May I return this pencil to its rightful owner?" he said with a slight tinge of irritation in his voice.

"It's mine, Professor Bathurst. I'm so sorry," said a voice next to Gayatri.

The professor offered the pencil back to its owner as if it were a wedding anniversary gift. Fina leaned over to see who had dared to let her pencil escape. She nudged Ruby and then rolled her eyes. It was Vera, of course. Vera Sapperton.

Ruby scribbled on Fina's notepad: "She's laying it on thick."

Fina nodded in agreement. But what could you expect from Vera-high-and-mighty-Sapperton? Her father was something big in the city. Pots and pots of money. And it showed. Though she did not flaunt her wealth, the cut of her clothes indicated her skirt alone had cost a mint. Vera had always been quite thin but her hands had become almost bony from additional loss of weight. Her lips were rouged in a perpetual raspberry-red, pouting to the point of caricature. Her extremely sparse eyebrows – all the rage at the moment – heightened this pouting effect. Fina thought she resembled a surprised clown, but not everyone else was of that opinion. Vera had suitors falling over her as if she were reeling them in on a fishing line. Her smouldering gaze and undulating gait ensured that was the case.

Lost in thought, Fina hadn't noticed the new instalment of Ruby's scribbles on her page. "We're designing evening gowns for her. I forgot to tell you."

Fina couldn't hold back what she knew was her own sour countenance. If Vera were simply a vapid rich girl, she wouldn't have a problem with her. The problem was that Vera was vicious. Yes, it ought to be her nickname, she thought. Never missed an opportunity to remind Fina of her father's murder and her brother's death. Viper.

She spent the remainder of the lecture staring at Professor Bathurst and doodling vipers in her notebook.

As Bathurst shut his lecture notebook with a bang, Fina was jolted into consciousness. Vera, Gayatri and Ruby all rushed to the lectern. Vera made it first, or rather she had decided she was going to be first in the queue.

Cocking her head to one side, she began to play with a twist of her long brown hair. She moved as close as was humanly possible to Bathurst, who clearly had no intention of backing away.

"Professor Bathurst, I wanted to apologise for dropping my pencil," she breathed. "It won't happen again."

"Not a problem, Miss Sapperton, not a problem," he said, chewing on a pencil of his own, which was covered in teeth marks.

Fina suppressed a laugh when she looked over at Gayatri and Ruby, patiently waiting behind Vera. Their mouths looked like cartoonish straight lines, as if Fina had drawn them herself.

"Please call me Vera."

Gayatri let out a whopping sigh.

Bathurst was unaware of, or didn't give a toss about, Gayatri's sigh. He replied, "You can call me ... Bathurst."

Ruby coughed, clearly covering her laugh.

Vera spun round at the sound of Ruby's laugh. She looked her up and down and then must have remembered Ruby was about to design her wardrobe.

"He's all yours, dearies," she said, throwing her handbag strap over her shoulder. But not before she gave Fina a look of ice-cold hatred as she sauntered out of the classroom.

As the cloud of Houbigant perfume left the room, Fina could breathe normally. She stayed back from Gayatri and Ruby as they introduced themselves to the new professor.

"As you know, we're both students of chemistry – though Gayatri plans to become a doctor," said Ruby, in a high voice Fina did not recognise.

He looked them up and down. "Tsk," he said, as if he were clearing out the remainders of breakfast from his front teeth.

Gayatri pressed on. "And we wondered, well, if we could be your research assistants in your laboratory. We've both had experience."

He flashed a winning smile at them. Then he held the smile in that artificial way one does when about to say something impolite. "I'm afraid I'm full up at the moment. And to be frank, I'm not sure you'd be up to the task. It's very demanding, high-level research," he said, finishing with a grunt.

Ruby clenched her jaw. Gayatri clenched her fist.

Fina narrowed her eyes on his face, as if she could will him to disappear.

Gayatri opened her mouth but Ruby pre-empted her. "I'm sure we understand, Professor Bathurst, that you think we're not up to the task."

Then the three of them marched out of the room, single file, not looking back.

4

The golden sunlight warmed the back of Fina's neck as she stood with Ruby and Gayatri on the steps of Wandesford Hall. Fina inhaled the sweet smell of freshly-cut grass on the quad. As they huddled together, Fina spied a nimble James Matua speeding down the stairs toward them.

"I say, it was a ripping lecture, what?" His eyes focused only on Gayatri. She tucked a wisp of hair which had escaped her plait behind her ear.

"It was alright," she said in response. Fina and Ruby murmured in agreement.

"But didn't you find the relationships between the ancient and the modern fascinating? I think I'll write about it in my political history paper," he said as his briefcase dropped to the floor. Fina bent over to pick it up. He looked at his watch and said, "Good Lord, I only have 24 hours to complete it!"

He was working on cultivating his absent-minded-professor routine early in his academic career, thought Fina.

"Yes, curse Professor Colveston's paper. I've finished it, though I need to review it once more," she said. "By the way, why were you in that lecture, James? You're a history student like I am, aren't you?"

He stiffened. "Oh, I thought I'd like to see what all the fuss was about – I mean, about him, about..." He trailed off. "What about you? Why were you there?"

A flash of heat spread across her face. "I came to keep these two company." Then she chided herself – why couldn't she say she wanted an eyeful of Professor Bathurst?

James relented. He looked somewhat ashamed and turned away, toward Gayatri. "Gayatri, are you ... have you been invited to Dean Ossington's annual sherry party yet?"

"Not yet. I assumed most senior students of Quenby would be invited. Why would you be interested, though? You're at a men's college."

He shifted his weight from side to side, nearly dropping his briefcase again. Why was the man so nervous?

"It's my mother. Before she left for New Zealand, where she met my father, she was a close friend of Dean Ossington's. So now the dean feels responsible for me, since it's my first year at college," he said, rubbing his chin.

Gayatri gave James a wide smile. It was a smile of sisterly affection. Perhaps not what James wanted, thought Fina. "Of course, I'll be there – if I receive an invitation from the dean. It's next week, right?"

"Yes. I'm not sure who the guest of honour will be."

"I hope it isn't as ghastly as last year's choice," said Ruby. "She was so dreadful I've driven her visage from my mind."

"Lady Aubyn-Tancred," put in Fina. "Yes, she was quite a treat. Felt like I was receiving an hour-long lecture from my great aunt about the dangers of what she terms 'involvement'."

James stared down at his feet.

Gayatri clearly sensed James would not be leaving unless she left as well. She gave him a little head bob after giving both Ruby and Fina a hug and then departed, with him in her wake.

"See how he trails after her like a little puppy," smiled Ruby.

"He has got it bad, as they say," agreed Fina. She turned back toward Ruby. "*Now* can you tell me what the postcard from Ian was all about?"

"Dearest Feens. I'm so sorry. Do forgive me."

Fina's exasperation melted away.

"You know it's because I worry. Fortunately, Bathurst was enough of a distraction that I didn't stew on it the entire lecture."

"Let's go to my room to have tea. I have some lovely biscuits sent to me by my mother. She buys masses of them from her favourite shop and then sends them to me whenever she wants me to call her."

The quad was quiet now as the students had all made their way to their next class. They walked at a leisurely pace toward their rooms in Tiscott Hall. Though she appreciated the imposing grandeur of the other college buildings, she found Tiscott eminently more inviting with its stout structure and cosy, curved windows that lined the compact quad.

Even though the walkway was empty, Ruby glanced around to make sure no one was in sight.

"As I said, the stamp means danger. Since he sent it to my address in college, I believe it means we ought to stay here."

"You don't think it means we should leave?"

"I thought about it, and I decided he wants us to 'lie low', as our American friends would say."

"Do you think someone is after us?"

Ruby blinked, but didn't reply.

"Selkies and kelpies. I suppose we have to be vigilant?"

"That's my life story, Feens. You know it," said Ruby.

Fina sighed and nodded. "Yes, I know. But what do we do? I

mean, do we just go about our normal business, or are there steps we need to take?"

"I think we're being watched by an agent. A British government agent or someone connected to British interests in the empire. The good news is it means we ought to just be ourselves – normal students, that is."

"We're not what you'd call normal, Ruby."

Ruby laughed. "So true, Feens. I suppose what I mean is we ought to go to class and involve ourselves in expected activities."

"Like going to a dreadful sherry party?"

"Exactly."

5

Despite its inviting exterior, Tiscott was a draughty building. Fina looked forward to a hot cup of tea. And biscuits, of course. Loads of lovely biscuits. She had worked up quite an appetite at the lecture. She deserved it.

Ruby's room was still warm from an earlier fire that had been reduced to ashes interspersed with bits of red glow. She marched over to her makeshift tea station on a side table and put on the electric kettle.

Fina threw off her shoes and folded them underneath herself as she settled into a worn but comfy chair.

"Do you think you can write to Ian to see if he can tell you more?"

Ruby poured the hot water into the teapot and placed it on the tray laden with edible goodness. She set it down in front of Fina, who sat in pleasurable anticipation of the tea and, more importantly, the biscuits.

"I did, but I'm afraid it won't reach him. At least not for a good while. As you saw from the photo on the postcard, he's in Grenada – but he didn't leave a forwarding address. I suspect it will be a few months before he returns to London. I did write to him there, but I made my wording even more vague – just in case someone is reading his mail while he is away."

Fina poured them each a cup of tea, enjoying the sounds of clinking spoons on their cups. She bit into a biscuit, which promptly dissolved into a pile of crumbs on her lap.

Ruby giggled. "Sorry, Feens. I told you my mum buys them all at once. I suspect they're a little stale."

"At least they still taste good," said Fina as she made a careful transfer of the crumbs onto a napkin. "I'll show you a trick. Put your mouth on the biscuit and blow warm air into it. I think the moisture makes the crumbs stick together."

"You ought to be a chemistry professor," Ruby said with a wink.

"In any case, back to our problem," said Fina, all business now that she had satiated the little brownie in her gut. "Is there anything else we can do?"

"Not really. I think we should be on the watch for anyone who acts particularly oddly around us."

"You mean like James?" smiled Fina.

"Oh, poor James. He is a bit gaga over Gayatri. I don't think she knows."

"Yes, or if she does, she's laying on the sister-love so he hopefully gets the hint."

"Doubtful," said Ruby. "Even if James were acting that way and wasn't smitten with Gayatri, I think his behaviour would be too obvious."

"I see. We're looking for a smooth operator."

"Precisely. Mind you, it could be we're safe by staying in college – and only have to worry if we leave." She shuddered. Then her face lit up. "I do have some good news, though. Wendell is coming to visit!"

"That's delightful!" replied Fina, who had developed a bond with Ruby's brother during her stay with the family in St Kitts. "When will he arrive?"

"Not until next week. In the meantime, I'm supposed to host a friend of his. Not that he can stay in college, but he is coming to meet up with Wendell. He's coming early to work on a story."

"He's a journalist? What's his name?"

"Pixley. Pixley Hayford. Have you heard of him?"

Fina's mouth dropped open. "Pixley Hayford? You must have heard of him. Remember the House of Lords story last year about an investment scheme gone off the rails?"

Ruby shook her head. "You know I only pay attention to the news when I have to. It makes my blood boil, so I try to avoid the daily news."

"Well, this was a stupendous scoop. If he's coming here to work on a story, it must be something quite juicy," said Fina. Her eyes lit up. "Perhaps I can interview him for one of my term papers on corruption!"

Sighing, Ruby said, "That's all we need. More attention drawn to ourselves. Still, I must be a good host. Wendell asked me to entertain him, though I told him how busy I was between schoolwork, designing new gowns for Vera—"

"Vera the Viper, you mean?"

"I know, but she pays! And she has so many friends in stuffy places. If I can get these few gowns correct, a whole new world will open for us. I hope you can help me out with the sewing as usual."

"Of course, I'd be happy to. Anything to avoid working on my next paper!"

After a few hours of distracted studying, Fina stepped out of her room to go to dinner. Even though it would take her no more than two minutes to reach the dining hall, she wrapped herself in a large woollen shawl. Shivering, she scurried down the corridor. She knew it wasn't that cold but the transition between the warmth of the summer and the chill of the autumn always affected her – to the point where she felt a little like her grandmother, complaining about her damp and draughty cottage on the Irish coast.

"Where are you off to in such a hurry, Miss Aubrey-Havelock?"

Fina turned round to behold a small woman, only a few years older than herself. She had the same little button nose as Fina. Her hair was a pile of curls trying to escape from the little linen cap on her head. Her smile looked genuine enough, though she was hunched over a broom as if it had been chaining her to the floor. Perhaps it had been. This must be the new college scout.

Fina made the first move. She strode over to the woman, hand outstretched. "How clever of you to know my name. You can call me Fina. You must be our new scout."

"Yes, miss. I'm Beatrice. Beatrice Truelove. Truelove by name, truelove by nature, says my gran."

"Welcome to Tiscott, Miss Truelove. I hope you've been finding everything you need. Have the other scouts been welcoming?"

"Oh yes, miss. They've been ever so kind, though I'm not sure about their cleanliness standards," she said with a sigh of resignation.

"Were you a scout at another college?"

"Oh no, miss, this is my first time being a scout. I was a maid for the Dowager Croxton at Trafford Manor," she said, swatting the air.

Fina didn't see any flies.

"Sounds grand. I'm off to dinner. Do let me know if you have any questions – sometimes the ladies around here can get rather high-spirited."

Beatrice nodded and began to sweep the corridor.

It was rather odd, thought Fina as she descended the square-spiral staircase. The corridor was already spotless.

6

Fina always felt at home in the small college dining room. They would occasionally sit at high table but she much preferred the casual, friendly atmosphere of their dining room. The round tables were conveniently pushed close enough together so one could hear gossip at the next table. It was also easy to get up from one table and move to another should you need to dine alone. Sometimes Fina did when she had to think.

The room was packed this evening, filled with lively chatter. Life was so full of possibilities this first week of the term. Even better, you could put off assignments without falling behind. Though she must begin her feudalism paper this weekend. Fina never liked bumping up against deadlines because they caused her tremendous anxiety. She wasn't particularly disciplined but did like to avoid staying up late to finish a paper. Though it had happened more than she cared to remember.

Gayatri sat next to Ruby in the corner. She patted the open seat next to her to signal to Fina it was free. Maud, the server and senior scout, was serving steaming dishes of artichokes in butter sauce and steak with crisped onions. Fina heard a growling.

"Was that my stomach?" she said, looking down.

Gayatri gave a little tinkling laugh Fina knew so well. "No, no, it was mine. Haven't eaten since breakfast."

Fina knew her own face expressed deep mortification at such a travesty. If she hadn't eaten since breakfast, she would – well, she wouldn't know where she'd be. Either shouting at some poor undeserving soul or laying prostrate in bed.

After the three of them had gobbled up their dinner in two minutes flat, they all leaned back in their chairs.

"Seconds?" asked Ruby, looking at her friends.

"Spiffing idea. Whenever Maud arrives again."

Now satiated, Fina could inspect the room properly. Vera reclined in one corner, looking fabulous in her black velvet lounge pyjamas with cream braiding. She was surrounded by a coterie of her so-called friends. Vera was the type of girl that attracted friends with such low self-esteem – such as Enid Wiverton – that they would attach themselves to a popular girl in the hopes her popularity would rub off on them. Fina had done that herself, so she was sorry for Enid. It always had the opposite effect. On the occasions when she'd tried to keep up with someone like Vera, she had always ended up feeling even worse about herself – even when the popular girl had had a somewhat bearable personality. Then there were the other "friends" who were essentially Vera's competition. They would play nice-nice, give each other air kisses and call each other *daw-ling*, but then would stab each other in the back as soon as they had a chance. Fina was sad about this, too. It all seemed like such a colossal waste of time.

She turned to the table nearest them, where Dean Ossington, Grace Yingxia and Professor Marlston had settled down for a late-ish dinner. The three of them had their heads together. Close. Very close. She could barely make out a few words here and there. Must be because they're in the presence of students, thought Fina.

Gayatri leaned over. "Since I just transferred from Somerville, I don't know who they are. Can you tell me?"

Fina leaned over toward her. "The one on the left in the lace and long pearl necklace is Dean Primrose Ossington."

Ruby leaned over so as not to be left out. "We call her Ossie, or sometimes Ossification ... because, well, she is old. Must be almost sixty!"

"Next to Ossie," continued Fina, "is Grace Yingxia. She is our poet-in-residence. It's a new position, tailored for her. She teaches occasionally. I've heard she invites students to teach with her in front of everyone. Can you imagine?"

Ruby finished the introductions. "And then next to Grace is Professor Victoria Marlston."

"She's my tutor in history," said Fina. "You wouldn't catch *her* asking students up to the podium. She's a bit strict and fussy, but I like her. She was apoplectic when I turned in a paper that was slightly wrinkled. A good lecturer, though."

Maud, a small spritely woman, came to their table with cheddar cheese and pie. "Are you ladies ready for the sweet? Cook made this with special apples from the kitchen garden this afternoon."

They nodded their heads in unison, forgetting the request for seconds of their meal.

Between slow bites of the sugary, tart apple with the palate-cleansing cheese, Fina listened intently to the conversation at the dean's table.

"He's the only one who can come at such short notice," said Victoria. The back of her chair was completely superfluous given her decidedly determined posture. She sat up straight but her head inclined over the table. It was the posture of someone who spent a great deal of time leaning over her desk. Every time she put down her fork, she placed it on the neatly folded napkin next to her plate, rather than on the plate. She must have two napkins. She performed the same operation with her knife, placing it next to the fork every time she took a mouthful of her meal.

"The man is a threat to decency everywhere," spat out Grace. The ballooning sleeves of her crimson chiffon blouse added drama to her emphatic gestures. It was as if her body language was perfectly in tune with the way the fabric of her clothes moved. Her taste in clothes ran just to the border of dramatic without stepping over the line into eccentric territory. Certainly not the eccentricity that would be accepted at Oxford.

"He's been very supportive of women's equality, Miss Yingxia. We mustn't forget that," said the dean in a slightly scolding voice.

Forks scraped against the dinnerware.

"And we mustn't forget he has become wealthy as a result of his fame," continued the dean. "He may make a generous donation to the college. Heaven only knows we could use additional funds right now."

"Well, I think we ought to cancel the whole event if he is our only option," said Grace.

"I tend to agree with Miss Yingxia," said Victoria. "Though I also know it will make us appear completely haphazard and disorganised to the rest of the university. That is something we cannot afford, especially because these two women's colleges are pitted against one another as if there should be only one."

"Right you are," said Grace.

"Well, that's settled then. We'll announce to the college tomorrow we've selected our guest speaker for the Luffnum Annual Lecture: Harold Baden Gasthorpe."

7

"I'm not going. And that's final," said Fina a few days later.

"I thought you were leaning toward going," said Ruby. "Don't you want to behold the Gasbag in all his vile glory? You could ask him some tough questions."

"Yes, but it's like feeding a tiger. You get too close and they'll bite you."

Ruby sighed, though not without a tone of irritation. Clearly, she knew better than to argue with Fina about something when her mind was made up.

"Something must have changed your mind, though," she said. She looked down at her watch. "We have that meeting with Dean Ossington soon. I do wish she would have let us know what it was about," she said, rubbing one forefinger in a vacant, automated way.

For once, Fina was not the one who was overly anxious. But that was only because she had more pressing matters on her mind.

"We have a few minutes before we need to be there. Let me show you the letter I received this morning," Fina said, removing a folded piece of paper from underneath the cat figurine on the mantel.

Ruby's eyes widened. "You know I don't like surprises," she said.

"I know, but I need you to read it. I've lost perspective on everything having to do with this blasted Luffnum lecture and sherry party."

Ruby unfolded the letter and read aloud:

Dear Miss Aubrey-Havelock:

I trust this letter finds you well.

I'm afraid I write to you with disturbing news. As the family solicitor, it is my duty to notify you if I believe your interests are threatened. And while I may be overreacting, I do believe caution is warranted in these circumstances.

Mr Harold Baden Gasthorpe visited my office approximately a week ago. I would not have met with him except for two facts. First, I knew his name from the papers, so I must admit I was intrigued to meet him. Second, and more importantly, he wrote a note explaining he wished to speak to me about your family's case. While this seemed rather peculiar, I did remember him using your family as an example of the ostensible wanton behaviour of the Irish.

After meeting and chatting with him, it became clear he had hoped to find out further information about your late brother. His gleeful behaviour indicated he already had heretofore unknown details about the case. Naturally, I declined to supply him with anything except a polite good-day and prompt escort out of my office.

Sincerely,

Reginald Tufton

If Fina weren't so upset by the letter, she would have enjoyed the rare look of total astonishment on Ruby's face.

"This Gasbag character certainly has a great deal of energy. Does he ever sleep?" said Ruby, letting her hand fall in her lap in a gesture of abject disgust. "What a cad."

"You see why I don't want to go to the lecture and sherry party? This awful man will publicly humiliate me, and will likely tell me more salacious particulars of my brother's case in public! Undoubtedly, it will be details I'd rather avoid."

Ruby sat up straight in her chair and then leaned over toward Fina. "I would think this letter would make you even more determined to see this pompous ass and tell him what you think to his face," she said in a low voice. "The Fina I know wouldn't shy away from being direct in the face of such a disgraceful personage."

Fina wavered. But the painful memories were already flooding back. She wanted to avoid that pain.

Ruby looked down at her watch. "You know I can go for you if you'd rather – then I can find out if he says anything. But either way, we must get a move on."

Fina leapt up like a jack-in-the-box. "Let's find out what Ossie has to say for herself," she said.

"Cracking idea, Feens," said Ruby with a grin.

~

DEAN OSSINGTON's college rooms were delightful. Though Fina was not a fan of lace herself – far too Victorian for her taste – she admired the way the curtains, doilies, and antimacassars adorned the room. In the centre sat the woman herself, decked out in her uniform: a frock adorned with white lace and a long strand of pearls. Ossie's birdlike eyes moved rapidly from side to side as Ruby and Fina took their seats opposite her in front of a cheerful fire.

Fina's tea was so hot she burned her tongue, nearly sending the cup flying into her lap. She counted it a small victory that the teacup did not escape her clutches, especially given the state of her nerves.

Ruby calmly sipped her tea and smoothed her hair. How could she drink it? Of course, thought Fina, peering over at her friend. She had put plenty of milk in her tea. Fina loved milky tea but often found it made it cold.

Dean Ossington set down her own cup of tea and folded her hands in her lap. "Thank you for coming, Miss Aubrey-Havelock and Miss Dove. I apologise for not notifying you of the subject of our conversation. The nature of the matter I wish to discuss with you is too delicate to discuss in public, and I was afraid you might inadvertently tell someone else about it," she said, clearing her throat. "And I made sure the college staff were out on errands so we could chat undisturbed."

She leaned over to hand Ruby and Fina a plate of bourbon biscuits. Fina's favourite. Ruby declined, but Fina expertly slid the closest one onto her saucer.

As Fina's mouth was full of biscuit, Ruby replied. "Yes, we're glad to be of assistance, Dean Ossington. We hope we haven't done anything to upset you."

The dean shook her head, causing her delicate pearl-drop earrings to spiral in little circles.

"No, no. Quite the opposite. Let me start from the beginning. A few weeks ago, I noticed certain items began to go missing from college."

"What kind of items?" asked Ruby.

"Precisely. What was odd was it began in the common areas. It's not unusual for students to walk off with a salt cellar or a glass. Usually, the staff find them in their rooms. But the staff came to me to tell me that other items, such as knick-knacks in the dining room, had begun to disappear. Slowly, one after another."

"Were they of any value?" queried Fina.

The dean sat back in her chair, squinting with what must have been the effort of remembrance.

"Not particularly valuable. Stealing them scarcely seemed worth the trouble."

"You said it *began* in the common areas. Did items from other areas go missing?" asked Ruby.

"Yes, and please remember this is highly confidential. If the upper administration of the university heard about this, it would be another excuse for them to persecute us as a women's college. We're already in enough trouble as it is..." she trailed off.

"Dean Ossington?" prompted Ruby, clearly hoping it would bring her back to the story at hand.

"Who has access to your rooms?" asked Fina.

"The scouts."

"Do you suspect one of them?"

Ossie paused, puckering her lips. "Well, all the scouts currently in college have been here for at least two or three years. Except Beatrice Truelove, of course."

Silence.

Ossie looked from Ruby to Fina, clearly expecting them to speak up. When nothing was forthcoming, she rattled on, "Naturally, the temptation must be considerable for women of that class—"

"Please, Dean Ossington," broke in Ruby, holding up her hand. Then, as if she realised she had just interrupted the dean, she continued, "Respectfully, a scout who dared to steal anything would naturally know they would be the first to be suspected. Not only because they have access to rooms in college, but because it would be assumed their status would compel them to steal."

Fina bobbed her head in rapid agreement. "Besides, other people could gain access. It would be easy enough to get into the staff rooms and take a set of extra keys."

"But it would likely have to be someone who had a reason to be in college so they could explain themselves," said Ruby.

"Yes. In American films, I believe they call it an 'inside job'," the dean sniffed.

Fina tried hard not to peek at Ruby because she knew she would laugh. It was difficult to imagine old Ossie at the pictures.

"Did anything else go missing from your rooms?" Ruby queried, ploughing ahead. She pursed her lips to suppress a fit of giggles.

Dean Ossington's lips quivered. "Well, there was a ring, with quite a valuable stone – I thought I'd lost it. And a few shillings disappeared from a box I had on a table near the door. And then..."

Ruby leaned forward. "I assure you, we'll keep this to ourselves."

"Very well. The thief stole my ... undergarments."

8

Ruby and Fina sat back in astonishment. Fina didn't know if she was more surprised by the fact the "undergarments" had disappeared or the fact that Dean Ossington wore undergarments. One just didn't consider...

"Yes," Dean Ossington said tersely. Then she moved to sweep crumbs off her lap, although it looked absolutely clean already.

"Why are you telling us this, Dean Ossington?" asked Ruby. "I'm sure Fina and I are flattered, but I'm not sure why you want us to know." A note of caution crept into her voice. "You don't think we know anything about it, do you?" Ruby's jaw clenched.

"Oh no, dears. No, no. Nothing of the sort. I'm so sorry," said the dean, shaking her head absently. "I've heard you two are sleuths of a kind."

Ruby froze. Fina could see she was unable to respond, so she gave it a go. "Where did you hear that, Dean Ossington?" she said in her most casual voice, even though she knew it sounded forced as she said it.

"Gayatri Badarur."

Now Ruby's fist had formed into a little ball.

Fina cleared her throat and stared into the dean's eyes. Ruby had taught her to watch the direction of someone's gaze to discern if they were lying. If they looked down to the left, it meant they were trying to think up a story.

"Gayatri. Why did she tell you that? Surely she didn't say something out of the blue," said Fina.

"Oh my," said the dean, not looking down at all, but straight ahead at Fina. "You must think her a frightful gossip. You must not think ill of her. You see, she had items stolen as well. Some of her chemistry set – from the laboratory, and a necklace, and, well, her underclothes as well. She didn't know who to turn to. At first, she thought someone had taken her chemistry set by accident. But then when her underclothes went missing..."

"Yes, it would be hard to misplace those, though I suppose it must have been more than a lost sock from the laundry."

Dean Ossington nodded.

"So you see, she came to me. Then I told her my story. We decided if the two of us – who have little in common otherwise – had been targets of the thief, then there must be others in college who are simply too embarrassed to come forward." She licked her lips and continued. "Miss Badarur told me she knew you two had luck solving other types of mysterious occurrences – though she was too discreet to tell me what they were. We thought it would be best to go to you two first before we took any other steps."

Ruby had relaxed by now. Her back was still quite straight but her muscles had loosened considerably.

"Yes, I can see that," said Ruby. "Thefts in a women's college would cause quite a stir, but if the underclothes detail were to become known..."

"Precisely. It would be proof we're either sex-starved man-haters or that we're not safe being in college."

Fina stared at the dean. Had the woman said the word "sex"? Surely not. Not Ossie. She was distracted from her usual internal monologue by Ruby standing up to pace by the fireplace. Fina grinned. This pacing must mean they were going to take "the case", as it were.

Ruby looked at Fina. "Fina – are you game for this adventure?"

Fina nodded. "Of course!"

"Splendid, ladies," said the dean, rising to her feet.

Ruby came to a halt and swirled around in her A-line tweed skirt. "Before we say yes to helping you find out the source of these thefts, I do have one condition."

"Yes, dear?"

Fina winced at the "dear", although it was easier to stomach from the dean.

"If we find out the reason for these thefts, and the identity of the thief, you must include us as equals in any decision about what will happen to her or him as a result," said Ruby.

"I suppose, but we'll have to turn her or him over to the police, won't we?" queried the dean.

"No, we don't. We'll cross that bridge when we come to it. Besides, isn't it better to handle it inside the college than to involve the police?"

"Perhaps..." wavered the dean. Then, looking resigned, she said, "Yes, I do agree to your conditions."

She cleared her throat and changed the subject. "Now, the only people who know about this in college are myself, Miss Badarur of course, yourselves, and the head scout who attends to my rooms. She only knows because staff have been telling her about the items stolen, and I also enquired about my missing ... linens, of course."

"Right," said Ruby. "We'll speak to Gayatri, and soon. Anything else you think we ought to do? Or anyone else we should speak to?"

"Well, I assume you're both attending the Luffnum Lecture

and sherry party. I believe it is vital you two are present, as most of the college will be there. I have a feeling in my bones our friend the thief might try to ply his trade at the sherry party. Perhaps the two of you could keep a careful eye on the guests."

Ruby nodded. "I agree. Though I do think it could be a woman or a man. From what you've told us, this thief has had increasing success. We don't know her or his motives, but it does seem like she or he may become overconfident. I propose we lay a trap."

"A trap?" said the dean and Fina in unison.

"Yes. Dean Ossington would arrange to have an item of value somewhere obvious in the room – on a ledge or mantel, for example. Then the three of us could watch to see if the thief dares to pilfer it."

Ossie shook her head. "I'm afraid I don't want anything to interfere with this sherry party. Harold Baden Gasthorpe is a potentially generous benefactor to the college. And we need all the funds we can secure to keep the college afloat. This trap of yours, Miss Dove, might prompt unpleasantness we can ill afford."

In a softer voice, she continued. "But I do appreciate the idea, Miss Dove. You two shall still be able to perform your sleuthing activities at the party, unbeknown to the other guests and Mr Gasthorpe."

Mr Gasthorpe. In all the talk of thief-catching, Fina had forgotten she would be drinking sherry with the odious man the next day. If they came face to face, she would even have to be polite to him, the "generous benefactor" to her beloved college. She managed to retain her composure as they said goodbye to the dean but outside her rooms her knees buckled.

Ruby grabbed her arm before she fell to the floor. "I'm so sorry, Feens," she said, hoisting her up and putting Fina's arm behind her shoulder. "But look at it this way. This case will be a welcome distraction from Gasbag's nonsense. We cannot give him too much power, right? Isn't that what my uncle told us when we were in St Kitts this spring?"

Fina unhooked herself from Ruby and nodded bravely. "Yes, you're right. I'll do it. And who knows, if he provokes me enough, I'll sock him good and proper!"

"That's the spirit, Feens!"

9

The next morning disproved the ominous forecasts of a storm. The world was still and quiet.

Fina had slept fitfully the night before, throwing her bedclothes off and on. Nightmares plagued her sleep. Finally, at 4:30, she arose and decided it was better to get some work done before the sun rose on this dreadful day. The day of the Gasbag. No, she mustn't think like that. There were plenty of pleasant things to anticipate. Meeting this new Pixley character coming in by train this afternoon and the thrill of another case with Ruby. She thanked her lucky stars it was a simple theft rather than murder.

Still groggy, she switched on the kettle and went over to the window. She liked to see if lights were on at this hour. It made her feel like she had a bond with that person. All the windows were dark, but she saw a figure scurrying across the quad. Fina squinted, trying to make out who it might be at this time of night. She couldn't be sure but the figure did seem to resemble the new scout – Beatrice. Or Beatrice Truelove, as she would say. What the devil was she doing out this late? Perhaps she was tending to a student who was ill.

Her momentary puzzlement faded away with the steam of the kettle. Hmmm ... if only she had something to eat. She shook the biscuit tin, even though she was certain it was empty. The powdered milk in her tea would have to tide her over until breakfast.

Sipping her tea, she peered out of the window again and then sat down at her desk to work. She only got up when she heard signs of life in the corridor as other students went to bathe and ready themselves for the morning. She couldn't believe how focused she was, nor how much she had completed. It was a gift from her mind. She'd been sure she would be too distracted to work.

After taking a warm bath – another benefit of getting up early was access to hot water – she prepared for the day. She laid out the peach velvet gown she would wear at tonight's party, so she wouldn't have to make that difficult decision later. Then she slid into her favourite teal day dress and a low-heeled pair of white shoes. Feeling comfortable now, she carefully prepared her bag with everything she'd need: pencil, notebook, brush, lipstick, journal, and a tin of mints. She looked around for her favourite chain with a tiny locket, but couldn't find it in her jewellery box. As her chest tightened in rising panic, she told herself to breathe. Had the college pilferer made a victim of her, too?

Fina thought back, picturing the previous night. Her photographic memory was her saviour she thought as she located the necklace in her nightstand drawer.

Now she was ready to face the day.

After ploughing through a substantial breakfast and then attending morning lecture, Ruby and Fina met to retrieve Pixley from the train station.

While they were waiting on the platform, Ruby mused, "I can't help wishing there was a way we could persuade Ossie to set a trap for the culprit. There must be something she could put out that the thief simply couldn't resist."

"Such as women's underclothes?" said Fina with a giggle.

"Perfect – right in the centre of the mantel," said Ruby with a belly laugh.

As they stood laughing on the platform, they saw a small, bald figure stride toward them with a purposeful step. Though he was rather petite, Fina could see muscles bulging under the arms of his sharp, open-necked dark grey suit. This must be Pixley Hayford. She approved of his black-framed round spectacles.

"Miss Dove?" he said, dropping his suitcase to shake Ruby's hand while placing the other over it.

Ruby cocked her head to one side. "Why yes, you must be Mr Hayford. How did you know who I was?"

"Please call me Pixley. Wendell showed me a photograph and he also said there was a strong family resemblance. And there is, most certainly," he said, looking at her appreciatively.

"I see. Do call me Ruby ... I've been dying to ask you about your name. May I be so bold?"

He smiled. "Let me guess. You want to know if I was named after Pixley ka Isaka Seme – the barrister trained at Oxford and founder of South African Native National Congress? The answer is yes, my father knew him when he was admitted to Oxford to read law."

"That is indeed a lot to live up to! But I see you're well on your way," said Ruby graciously. She gestured toward Fina. "This is Fina. Fina Aubrey-Havelock. My best friend."

Fina glowed in the warmth of her title as *best friend.*

They exchanged the usual pleasantries as they walked from the station back to college. As it was almost an hour before the lecture was set to begin, they agreed to meet Pixley back at the pub below his rooms in the local inn – the Peacock and Parrot – before they made their way to the lecture together.

Twenty minutes later, Fina and Ruby found themselves in a pleasant and blessedly quiet local pub. The three of them studiously ignored stares from the locals. Fina ordered a cider while Ruby ordered a pint of bitter.

"Ah," said Fina. "This cider was a topping idea. It calms my nerves," she said, now feeling more optimistic about how this evening was going to unfold.

Gesturing with his pint glass at Fina, Pixley said, "Ruby caught me up on the details of your relationship to Gasthorpe, though I guess you'd scarcely call it a relationship."

"You're correct. I'd call it an antagonism. And if you hear me refer to "Gasbag" during the evening, it is my thinly veiled reference to that odious man."

"Fair enough," he said, taking a long draught from his glass.

"I have to say I am a Pixley Hayford enthusiast," said Fina. This cider was very tasty, she thought. She looked at Ruby, whose face resembled someone waiting for an accident to happen. No matter; she was in complete control of her faculties. "I followed your most famous story last year about corruption. And I've also been following your series on the Italian invasion of Ethiopia in the *Manchester Sentinel*. Quite marvellous." Fina hiccoughed. "Excuse me. Not that the invasion was marvellous."

"I quite understand," Pixley said. He had removed his spectacles and was twirling them around, perilously close to his glass.

Fina thought she'd better change the subject. "Are you here to visit Wendell only or is there a reason you travelled down earlier? Are you following a story?"

"You are direct, aren't you?" he said with a mischievous grin. "Yes, I'm following a few different leads. None of them are solid, you understand, but there were enough of them that I thought this lecture and event would give me an idea if I ought to pursue any of them further."

"So you're kind of like a spy, aren't you?" she said, without malice. "Ruby and I—" but before she could finish her sentence, Ruby had placed a hand over hers in a clear signal to be quiet.

And quiet she was.

10

Thunderous applause rocked the lecture hall.

One student rose. Then another. Soon, most of the crowd were on their feet, cheering, clapping and thumping.

Fina and her friends stayed glued to their seats. If any of them were inclined to give in to peer pressure by participating in the standing ovation, a quick look of fury from Fina stopped them in their tracks. She had spent most of the lecture staring at various points in the hall. First, the salt-and-pepper head directly in front of her, which had the irritating habit of nodding agreement periodically. Then she gazed at the lit candles in the corner, flickering whenever a new audience member opened the door to enter. She had watched the wax burn and drip in rivulets down the candleholder. From time to time, she heard parts of phrases, such as “the English people are the pinnacle of civilised progress”. And, “the mark of the inferiority of the Irish is their treatment of women”. The last bit she heard was, “the great British Empire provides all we need to feed the masses here at home”.

The hall had been as stuffy as the lecture, thought Fina, as

Ruby, Pixley, Gayatri, and Wendell congregated on the steps outside the lecture hall. Too much hot air.

"Good Lord," said Pixley. "Was that not the most ghastly claptrap you've ever heard? What was all that rot about the English working classes propping up the colonies? More like the reverse."

"I suppose we can be grateful he supports women's equality," said Gayatri, ever the apparent optimist.

Ruby coughed. Her visage was one of disbelief. "Hardly equality for the likes of you and me, Gayatri."

"I suppose you're right. His discussions of India were utter rubbish," said Gayatri. Looking at Fina, she said, "And Ireland." And then, looking at Ruby and Pixley, she added, "And the Caribbean."

"Don't stare at me," said Pixley. "My grandparents came to London from Ghana in the seventeenth century. Though I do have an interest in anti-colonial fights."

Fina gave Ruby a gentle nudge. Without looking over at her, Ruby gave a slight nod. Could Pixley be provoking them? Surely not. Wendell wouldn't have sent him down if there was any chance he could be spying on them.

Hitching her dress slightly to descend the stairs, Ruby said, "Time to go to the dreaded sherry party."

THE LEVEL of chatter emanating from the great oak doors of the senior common room indicated the sherry party was well under way. Guests spilled out into the hall and Fina was quite sure many were taking advantage of the balcony in the front, despite the chill in the air.

As if she were steeling herself to enter a particularly difficult exam room, Fina took gulps of air and unconsciously held her breath as they entered. Gayatri took the lead and the little party followed her like a trail of baby ducklings as she cut a swathe through the crowd.

"Topping idea, Gayatri," said Fina when they finally arrived at their destination: the drinks table. Fina noticed Ruby give her a worried look so she settled on a ginger beer rather than sherry. Gayatri and Ruby both decided on glasses of bubbly, while Pixley preferred wine. So much for a sherry party.

Fina sipped the ginger beer and wrinkled her nose. Too sweet. But the bubbles were refreshing in her throat. A few feet away, she saw Professor Marlston had made the same drink choice. She stood next to Grace Yingxia, who held a rapidly disappearing glass of champagne in her hands. Fina reflected that they were an odd couple indeed. They both had good posture but where Grace's was the easy poise of the confident, Victoria Marlston held herself in an enforced rigidity. Her head was the only body part out of alignment: it always stooped forward a bit. She held her ginger beer so tightly Fina thought she might shatter the glass. Grace, on the other hand – true to her name – held her champagne glass with a light, feathery touch.

Feeling rather emboldened by the lingering effects of her earlier alcohol consumption, Fina floated – or at least it felt that way to her – toward the pair. They clinked their glasses in salute.

Grace turned to Fina. "Did you enjoy the lecture? Or perhaps a better Oxford question would be, 'Did you find it edifying?'"

Fina decided it was safe to share her thoughts with the two of them. "I found it to be the most irritating, nonsensical drivel I've ever heard!" she said, with a little more fervour than she'd intended.

"Please, tell us what you really think," said Grace with a wink. "You're right, of course. I found my mind wandering during the lecture. Which I must say is not unusual, even if I enjoy the content." She unsnapped her black clutch and pulled out the tiniest leather-bound notebook Fina had ever seen. It had an equally tiny pencil attached to it on a loop of thread. Grace fanned the pages as if it were one of those flip books which make it look like you're watching a moving picture. The pages were filled with notes. "I like to jot down ideas for poems whenever I'm in a tiring situation."

"The only problem with your system, dear Grace, is you lose those wonderful notebooks left and right," said Victoria with a grimace. "Just the other day, I found one on the floor of my office."

"I'm sure you scooped it right up, darling, given your penchant for order," smiled Grace. It was not a sarcastic remark. It struck Fina as the type of remark her grandmother would say to her grandfather – a gently chiding but loving remark of a couple who had lived together for more than a few years.

Grace held her hand to her forehead in the rather theatrical manner of a fortune-teller. "An idea has arrived. I must dash," she said, grabbing her clutch and twirling off in a fairy-like motion toward the balcony. Professor Marlston gave Fina a little nod of polite excuse and tramped off after her friend.

Fina felt the presence of someone behind her. "I say, how long have you been at Oxford?" Pixley enquired above the din. Fina was sure he was being polite. She motioned to the group to decamp to a recess near the balcony.

"Ah, that's better," said Fina to Pixley, as a cool, gentle breeze ruffled her hair. "To answer your question, I've been at Oxford for two years."

Nodding, he continued his inquisition. "And you like Quenby College? What made you choose Quenby over Somerville?"

"Is this a professional interrogation, or simple human interest?"

Pixley took a little bow. "Sorry, it's a rather nasty professional habit, as you say. I start interviewing everyone I meet. Please forgive me."

"No harm done. And I chose Quenby because, well, it was the more progressive of the two colleges."

He raised his glass to her in a salute. She raised hers to clink his.

"Now it's my turn," Fina said, hoping he had imbibed enough to loosen his tongue. "Won't you give us a hint as to what story – or stories – you are following while you're here?"

Pixley shifted his weight from side to side and then made a little jumping motion like a boxer preparing for a fight.

"Well..."

"Perhaps you can tell me if it's about individual people or the college itself?" She was warming to this guessing-game format of conversation.

"The college."

"Really?" Ruby had joined their conversation by now. "Let's see, is it about politics, money, sex, jealousy or...?"

"Well, you know my area of interest. And it isn't sex and jealousy. Though I am rather taken by that man over there," he said, casually waving his glass in the direction of the grand piano.

"You're not the only one," sighed Fina. "That's Professor Esmond Bathurst, the new chemistry professor. This is his first term teaching at college."

"To put it politely, Pixley," said Ruby, "the man is a boor."

"Such a pity. What a waste of a fine physique," said Pixley, still staring at Bathurst. "Who is the young woman talking to him? The two of them are as thick as thieves. I know I shouldn't judge a book by its cover but that one looks like trouble."

"You're not far wrong, unfortunately," replied Fina. "That's

Vera the Viper. She is positively spiteful. I would feel sorry for her if she weren't rolling in it."

"Speaking of which, Feens," said Ruby, touching her shoulder, "we have to meet with her tomorrow about her new wardrobe."

"Might as well pack this week with all the unpleasantness possible. It will make next week seem like a positive picnic."

Pixley made another motioning gesture toward Enid, who was perched on a stool at the other end of the room.

"Who is that? Shall we find out what her story might be?" he asked. With Fina in his wake, he toddled toward Enid and introduced himself. The trio clinked their glasses in salute.

"Enjoying the party?" asked Fina.

"I suppose. As much as I ever enjoy parties," said Enid, clearing her throat.

Fina surveyed the girl. Her shoulders drooped and she fidgeted with her sherry glass, twisting it round and round. She directed a trance-like stare at Vera and Esmond. The glass spun faster and faster. Fina thought it might splatter all over Enid's Argyle jumper.

As Fina continued to watch Enid, she found that she couldn't tell if she were staring at the couple or at Ruby. Her stomach gave a little lurch – what if she were watching Ruby?

Pixley peered at Enid, and then his eyes darted in the direction of her stare. "Have you met Ruby Dove before? We could introduce you if you haven't."

Enid gave Pixley a half-squint. "Who? Oh. Ruby. I've met her," she said, sliding off her stool.

"Please excuse me," she said, moving toward Vera.

"Peculiar. Distinctly peculiar," said Pixley, turning to Fina. "I knew someone like that once. Completely lost in her head – not intellectually, but emotionally, you understand. Would moon about all day, staring at different people. I suppose Freud might call it repressed, but that doesn't capture the complexity of the condition. It didn't end well, I'm afraid."

"Was she institutionalised?" asked Fina with a shudder. She promptly downed the remainder of her ginger beer as if it would have the relaxing effect of alcohol.

Pixley twirled his spectacles again, apparently lost in memories. He looked up and put on his spectacles.

"In a manner of speaking, I suppose. She committed murder."

11

"Another drink, Miss Aubrey Havelock?" said Beatrice, proffering a tray full of sherry.

"Mhm, they look delicious, but I'd better not. Thank you, Beatrice. How are you getting on?" Fina enquired.

"Just fine, miss. Quite the party, isn't it?" Beatrice said, looking admiringly out over the din. The crowd had thinned a bit. "Which one of the guests is Mr Gasthorpe?"

Fina waved a shaking hand in the direction of a doughy man in a blue serge suit near the doorway. His choice of clothing was infuriating – not because of the clothing itself, but because it was supposed to indicate Gasthorpe was a "man of the people", although his suit was clearly Savile Row.

"That man does like his pipe," said Beatrice. "He's constantly topping it up." She shook her head in disapproval. Perhaps she was afraid of the mess created by constantly filling one's pipe.

Wanting to steer the conversation away from the Gasbag, Fina said, "I woke up early this morning. I thought I saw you in the quad. You must be quite a diligent scout to get up that early."

Beatrice's curls began to tremble and the tray cocked itself at a rather dangerous angle as she still stared at Gasthorpe. Fina raised the tray, almost imperceptibly, to avoid disaster.

"Oh, it wasn't me, miss. That must have been someone else you saw," she said hurriedly. She licked her lips. "I see Dean Ossington is waving to me by the fireplace. Excuse me, miss, I must find out what she wants."

She scuttled off toward the fireplace. Her white cap escaped and fell to the floor. Fina retrieved it and joined the dean by the fireplace. After she had returned the cap to its rightful owner – who immediately rushed off to another corner of the room – she turned to Dean Ossington.

"Lovely party, isn't it?" said the dean.

Resplendent in navy lace, contrasting nicely with her pearls, the dean sipped her glass of sherry. She seemed to be one of the few who partook of the sherry.

"Mhm," was all Fina could manage to reply. She looked over at the corner where her friends were still lounging. Ruby was clearly half listening to Pixley and half watching Fina. James Matua had joined the party and had cornered Gayatri with grand hand gestures.

"You know, Miss Aubrey-Havelock, this party is going so well that I do believe Mr Gasthorpe might give the college some of the funding we so sorely need. You know he fully supports women's equality."

"Really?" Fina knew her one-word replies were not what was expected of the rarefied intellectual atmosphere of Oxford, but it was all she could manage at the moment.

Dean Ossington leaned over with a conspiratorial glance around the room. "I've decided to take Miss Dove's advice ... about a trap," she said in a hushed voice.

Fina leaned in closer. "What made you change your mind?"

The dean smiled and nodded out at the crowd as if they were chatting about a light and relatively vapid subject. "A very valuable silver cow creamer was stolen from one of the common rooms. We keep it in a glass case, but never worried about anyone taking it. It's worth a great deal, but you wouldn't necessarily know just by looking at it. Its value derives not only from the silver, but from the fact it is a rare antique."

"A cow creamer?" asked Fina to no one in particular. "Ah, now I remember. It was in a curio case in the corner of the largest common study room, correct?"

"Exactly. I decided Miss Dove's supposition about the increasing bravery – or hopefully carelessness – of our college pilferer demanded more decisive action. Observe the fireplace mantel, Miss Aubrey-Havelock. There are a number of worthless knick-knacks on it, but there is one item of real value. Can you identify it?"

Fina squinted at the mantel. She saw a photograph framed in what looked to be wood, a bronze carriage clock, a porcelain figurine, and another wood-framed picture, though this appeared to be some sort of certificate. "I don't know, Dean Ossington. Perhaps the carriage clock?"

Another voice chimed in. "What carriage clock? The carriage clock of time, what?"

Fina turned back toward the dean to see the new arrival. She was surprised she could manage even that at the sound of that voice. Gasbag.

"Dear Miss Ossington—" he said rather unctuously.

"It's Dean Ossington, if you don't mind, Mr Gasthorpe," she said firmly.

He gave her a look of mock surprise. Then he chomped on his pipe. This man was simply the end. The end.

"So sorry, *Dean* Ossington. Have you met my personal secretary, Jack Devenish?" he said, placing one hand casually on his secretary's shoulder. Fina had seen the man during the lecture, but couldn't quite figure out what role he played in the Gasbag show. Tall, with thinning sandy hair, he had the appearance of a man who had gone to seed before his time. He wore a loud checked suit which Fina could have appreciated as edgy if worn in another context, along with a rather garish tie which appeared to have little racing cars speckling the front of it.

He stuck out a hand to Dean Ossington as if he were ready to sell her some rather dubious housecleaning products. "Pleased to meet you, Dean Ossington," he said with an affable grin. He said "Dean" as if it were her first name, rather than a title. Must stop judging, Fina admonished herself. But she couldn't help it – anyone associated with Harold Baden Gasthorpe was bound to receive rather poor marks from Fina. There was something odd about the man, aside from that, however. His overly forward, affable manner. It was rather ... American. At least in her head it was American. Fina hadn't met too many Americans in person, and so most of her images came from films.

"And who is this lovely lady?" asked Devenish of Dean Ossington as if he were enquiring about the name of a child's favourite toy. Definitely a tinge of an American accent.

"I'm Fina Aubrey-Havelock," she said simply, offering her hand to him out of forced politeness. She reminded herself she was being kind for the dean as well as the college.

She turned slightly on her heel to observe Gasthorpe's face. He had puffy eyelids and slightly bloodshot eyes. Little wonder given his immense productivity – too bad he couldn't be a little less prolific.

He stopped in the middle of inserting more tobacco into his pipe from a small tin he had taken from his pocket.

"Well, Miss Aubrey-Havelock. Pleased to meet you face-to-face. I've heard a lot about you. Or I ought to say, I've heard it mostly secondhand when I was researching your brother's case," he said, gently taking her hand from her side. He had a slightly adenoidal tinge to his voice that made him even more irritating.

"Yes, I've found out some very interesting information about your family."

"Mr Gasthorpe, I—" intervened Jack.

"Calm yourself, Jack, I can handle this," he retorted.

Fina snatched her hand away. She blurted out, "May the devil make a ladder of your backbone and pluck apples in the garden of hell!" Seizing one of the nearby half-full sherry glasses, she splattered the contents in his face. His bulging eyes and blotchy face prompted her to take further action.

She socked him in the jaw.

He tipped over backwards like a set of dominos.

12

In the now-empty corridor, Fina wiped away her hot tears. Ruby was at her side, offering her another handkerchief.

"Why'd you do it, Feens?"

"He said he had more information about my family. And was, well, being a pompous ass in general."

"I have to admit I'd have a hard time just standing there and listening to that, too." Then Ruby began to laugh. Laugh so hard she doubled over.

"What's so funny?" asked Fina, momentarily distracted from her troubles.

"I was remembering the time you slapped that woman – Emeline! On the trip to Port of Spain in the spring. I had wished at the time I had been there to see it. Now I've seen it in person. Will you be my personal guard, Feens?"

Fina blinked. Then the absurdity of it all made her laugh as well. Soon the two of them were both doubled over in a kind of giddy, trance-like laughter.

"What are you doing?" Gayatri demanded. She was partially obscured by a stand bulging with coats. Pixley and James also emerged from behind the mass of outerwear. They all had looks of extreme horror on their faces.

Wiping away the tears of laughter, Ruby replied, "You must admit, it was quite funny. Gasthorpe got what was coming to him – a right biff in the jaw."

Gayatri and the others lost their horrified expressions. Now they looked rather awkward and uncomfortable. Another figure emerged from behind the coats. Dean Ossington.

"Fina Aubrey-Havelock!"

Oh dear, thought Fina. Her mind raced while she weighed the options. Should she be horrified by her own actions and fall all over herself to be contrite? Or play the vindicated victor?

As Fina clearly looked like a squirrel caught in the act of hiding its nuts for winter, Ruby made the decision for her.

"Dean Ossington, I cannot speak for Fina, but I imagine whatever he said about Fina's family was too much to bear."

The dean marched over to Fina. She bent over and whispered, "You must apologise. Please, do it for me. Do it for the college."

Standing up again, the dean said to Ruby, "I do agree the girl has spirit," she said with a grudging grin. "But beware if you tell anyone I think so. We still have to play nice with Mr Gasthorpe. Remember, he supports women's education. I'm not sure he'll make a cheque out to us after this ... incident," she said sadly.

Fina was still bent at a slight incline, not from laughter, but from a queasiness that had descended on her. She began to grasp the reality of the situation.

She looked up at the dean. "I will apologise, Dean Ossington. I need a few minutes to myself before I do so."

Fina threw cold water on her face and stared at the mirror in the bathroom. It was blessedly empty. Her hair was a frizzy mess, and her eyes were so puffy she thought she almost looked like Gasthorpe himself. She did her best to brush her hair and take a few deep breaths. Then she said aloud to herself – even though she felt self-conscious about it – "You can do it, Fina."

Back in the senior common room, Fina saw the only guests who remained were Ruby, Gayatri, Pixley, James, Professor Bathurst, Vera with Enid Wiverton, the dean, Grace Yingxia, and Professor Marlston. And Beatrice, who was clearing away drinks in the corner. Jack Devenish and Dean Ossington were huddled in a corner by the piano with Gasthorpe, who was rubbing his eyes painfully hard. All the guests turned toward Fina when she entered – as if she were an apparition. Most of them had the grace to be embarrassed by their staring and turn away.

Now or never, thought Fina to herself.

She marched up to the trio in the corner by the piano. "Mr Gasthorpe, I– I– I–"

Gasthorpe turned toward her, eyelids twitching. Then his mouth began to work. Then his whole body. He coughed and made a strangled noise, leaning on Jack Devenish, who was doing his best to hold him up.

Then he tumbled to the floor. Only then did his pipe fall loose from the clutches of his lips.

13

"Selkies and kelpies," breathed Fina.

"Indeed, Feens," said Ruby as a small crowd had formed around Gasthorpe's prostrate body.

Jack Devenish squatted next to the body, felt for a pulse. He shook his head and then slid his hand over Gasthorpe's eyelids. That fish-like stare Fina had seen before was too much for her.

"I'm afraid we'll need to call for the police."

"But why, Mr Devenish?" asked Dean Ossington. "He must have died of some sort of fit – or a heart attack."

"I'm afraid not. I worked as a medic in the war. I'm afraid Mr Gasthorpe has been poisoned."

At the word "poison", the chemistry experts in the room – more than your average percentage, thought Fina – closed in around the body.

"What kind of poison?" Esmond demanded.

Jack goggled at the body. "I don't know, but it does look like poisoning." He turned to stare at Beatrice, who had dropped her serving tray on the floor in the commotion. "Miss," he said to her, "please stop tidying up. Everything in this room is evidence."

Dean Ossington said she would telephone the police from the hall. Ruby whispered to Fina, "There's no way to avoid the police this time."

Ruby, Gayatri and Fina sat down in a corner. They all stared at the floor. Waiting. Slowly, the possible consequences of this murder began to dawn on Fina. Surely everything would be alright. Images of the police coming to her home after her father's murder swelled up in her thoughts. She couldn't endure that again, and what if they thought she did it? As these thoughts began to spiral out of control, she looked over at Ruby. Ruby sat very still, posture erect, hands in lap. She was clearly steeling herself for dealing with the police. Ruby had only mentioned in passing her encounters with them in the past. Though she was never specific, Fina knew her friend well enough to know they had been traumatic – and that she didn't want to discuss them further.

Gayatri, too, sat still. Her countenance was different to Ruby's, however. Her eyes were closed and she leaned right back against the chair. Fina touched her gently.

"Gayatri," she whispered. "You were the one who told Ossie about our investigation skills."

Gayatri quickly squeezed Fina's hand. "I'm so sorry, but it seemed like the right thing to do," she said in a low voice. "I didn't tell her anything about what happened at Pauncefort, I promise."

Ruby intervened, also whispering. "Then we all have to promise not to say anything about the college thefts – unless we absolutely have to."

The three of them nodded in unison, making a silent pact.

Fina noticed everyone else was huddled in small groups, exchanging sporadic and desultory words.

"Real tragedy. Such a fighter for the common man – and for women, too."

"I do hope this won't take too much longer. I need my beauty sleep."

"Golly, do you think they'll close the whole college tomorrow?"

After what seemed an eternity, but was surely only twenty minutes, Fina heard rapid footsteps, like a small band of excited ponies. She glanced over at the mantel to see the time.

The carriage clock had vanished.

Three figures entered the room, one in a police uniform, the other in a dark grey suit, and the third, and tallest, in a brown suit and a homburg.

The one in the brown suit trundled over to Esmond and Jack Devenish. The only white men in the room, of course, thought Fina, acidly.

"Dean Ossington?" he said to Esmond in his professorial regalia.

"Afraid not, Chief Inspector," he said, peering at the badge the man proffered. "Dean Ossington is sitting on that sofa," he said, pointing to the hunched figure of Dean Ossington. Poor Ossie, thought Fina. She looks positively crushed.

Dean Ossington rose to meet the police officer. "I'm Primrose Ossington, dean of this college," she said.

Shaking hands, he replied, "Chief Inspector Hogston, Oxford City Police."

Despite herself, Fina gave out a little snort. Contrary to his name, Hogston more closely resembled a weasel. Fina had never seen anyone with such spotless white teeth. He must either have dentures or be a compulsive tooth-brusher, she thought absently. She guessed he must be around forty, while the two officers he had in tow must be closer to her age.

Waving his hand like a magician about to make a rabbit appear, he gestured to the two police officers behind him. "This is Detective Sergeant Snorscomb," he said, pointing to the taller of the two. The only defining feature of Snorscomb was his pencil moustache. It was immaculate.

"And this," said Hogston, pointing to the man whose face was almost entirely obscured by his bobby helmet, "is Constable Clumber." Clumber hurriedly removed his hat and stood stock-still, as if he were under inspection himself. The transformation revealed someone who appeared to be a young woman. Curse her need to categorise people this way, Fina chided herself. No wonder Clumber hid underneath that hat – she could only imagine the level of harassment he would suffer in the hyper-masculine police force. He nervously withdrew matches from a matchbox, struck them and then blew them out. Fina watched him perform this operation at least four times.

This momentary distraction faded and Fina returned to the grim reality of the situation. After conferring in hushed tones with Dean Ossington, Hogston straightened up, held his hat over his heart and pronounced, "I'd like everyone to make short statements, please. We'll follow up with some of you tomorrow. Constable Clumber will attend to the crime scene while we all go to a common study room for a chat."

And with that, everyone began to gather their belongings. Hogston held up his hat and bounced a bit on the balls of his feet. "Please, leave all of your personal items here. You may retrieve them after we've finished questioning."

"Really, Chief Inspector. I have important papers I should not leave unattended," said Jack Devenish imperiously.

"Don't you worry. We'll attend to them," said Hogston in an even tone. A ghost of a smile lifted one corner of his mouth.

He led them out of the senior common room and into the hallway. Ruby caught up with Fina and said, "Just be calm and answer their questions. Don't be indignant." Fina nodded at her and gave her hand a reassuring squeeze.

When they arrived in front of one of the common study

rooms, Hogston said, "I'd like to speak to a Miss Fina Aubrey-Havelock first." He looked at the dean to make sure he had pronounced her name correctly.

Fina stepped forward. She could feel the eyes on her, which made her straighten her back even further and hold her head high. "Yes, Chief Inspector. I am she."

14

Fina sat facing the two police officers across a ridiculously small side table. They could have been at some nightclub act, waiting for the show to begin. Still, she was glad she had a barrier between them. Breathe deeply, she told herself. And she began to do so.

"Are you all right, Miss Aubrey-Havelock?" said Hogston. "You look as though you might faint."

Fina shook her head, which only made the room spin. She gripped the sides of the chair. "Well, Chief Inspector, I have had quite a turn."

He nodded sympathetically. Snorscomb removed a small notebook and pencil from his breast pocket. He smoothed his pencil moustache with a flourish and then flipped open the notebook. Carefully, he wetted the pencil with his tongue.

"Now, Miss Aubrey-Havelock. We decided to start with you because we fancied you might be the most distressed of the crowd—"

"Chief Inspector!" Fina was about to object to his presumption of her fragility. Then she thought better of it.

Hogston continued as if she hadn't said a word. "And we also know you had an altercation with the deceased a few minutes before he died."

Fina blinked. She wasn't going to explain herself without a direct question. All of her training with Ruby – and the others last summer in London – was beginning to come back to her. Thank heavens.

After a suitable pause for effect, Hogston continued. "Would you explain the precise nature of your disagreement with the deceased?"

The words tumbled out. Fina knew there was no use in hiding it, as most of her story was public in any case. It was best to tell them the truth.

Snorscomb scribbled furiously. Fina hoped he knew shorthand.

After she had completed her lengthy tale, Hogston said, "I understand you, ah, assaulted Mr Gasthorpe a few minutes before he died."

Her heart raced. Her palms became sweaty. All her relative calm washed away. "You can't think, Chief Inspector, you can't think that caused his death! He was poisoned!" She began to scan the room for an exit.

Snorscomb looked up from his scribbling.

"How do you know, Miss Aubrey-Havelock?" queried Hogston in a casual tone which carried a whiff of danger.

"Well, they all said he was poisoned!"

"*They*, Miss Aubrey-Havelock?"

"Professor Bathurst. And, what's-his-name. Gasbag's secretary."

"Did you say 'Gasbag', Miss Aubrey-Havelock?"

Fina could only imagine what her face looked like at this point. Her muscles ached as if she had been riding a horse all day.

"Ah, yes, Chief Inspector. It was a name I gave to Mr

Gasthorpe. You see, it helped me distance myself from him. Made him seem silly," said Fina, looking from one face to another with the hope one of them would show some understanding.

All she could see were blank faces. Snorscomb began to whistle, the kind of toothy whistle which almost sounds like buzzing. Hogston shot him a look of irritation. Snorscomb's whistle promptly transformed into throat-clearing.

He asked, "If you had such hatred of the man, why did you come to the party?"

Perfectly reasonable question. She supposed Ossington would have to tell them about the college thefts to explain why she was at the sherry party.

"You see, it was a special request from Dean Ossington." She paused, realising she'd have to explain Ruby was involved too. Damn and blast it. Double selkies and kelpies. "Dean Ossington..." She trailed off, considering what would happen if she told them *why* Ossie sought them out as investigators. Then that would involve Gayatri, Pauncefort Hall, Wendell, the murders in the Caribbean ... no, she couldn't take that risk. All she could do was hope Dean Ossington would have enough sense not to reveal their separate plan to investigate the thefts.

"Miss Aubrey-Havelock?" said Hogston, somewhat impatiently.

"Sorry, Chief Inspector. What I meant to say was Dean Ossington made a special request for more senior students to be at the party. She knew it would be difficult for me, but thought it was ... an important character-building exercise."

"I see," said Hogston, clearly unsure whether to press on this rather shoddy story. But this excuse might seem plausible to Hogston. After all, what did he know about the internal politics of a women's college?

Hogston leaned back in his chair, tipping it back on its hind legs. Snorscomb followed suit.

"You may think we don't know what's what, Miss Aubrey-Havelock. I've been on many cases at this university – though this is my first at a women's college. Came across some fool of a don who thought he could embezzle accounts without anyone noticing. Thought he could pull the wool over my eyes," he said, staring unblinkingly at Fina.

Then his chair came back to rest in its proper position with a clap.

"Miss Aubrey-Havelock. I'm afraid we will have to detain you until we receive definitive notice about the cause of death. Right now, all evidence points to the possibility of a delayed brain haemorrhage from the fall caused by your assault."

Pinpricks of sweat made her itch all over. Her stomach turned into a brick. She could only manage a few words. "Please tell Ruby Dove. Please tell her."

15

After a gruelling night, Fina awoke heavy-headed, unable to wipe the memory of her time at the police station from her mind. Chief Inspector Hogston had kept her there for two hours, without so much as a cup of tea, grilling her about her so-called 'feud' with Gasthorpe, her family history, her allegedly hair-trigger temper...

She was saved only by the entrance of Constable Clumber with the pathologist's preliminary report. Hogston flipped through the pages.

"Hmmm. Well, Miss-Aubrey-Havelock, this may be of interest to you." He paused and looked up to gauge her reaction. Get on with it, pleaded Fina silently.

"It seems Mr Gasthorpe did not die from the assault. He died from poison, though we are not yet sure what kind of poison."

Fina's shoulders sagged with relief. "Does that mean I can go?"

"Yes," said the inspector. "For now," he added pointedly.

~

Over breakfast at her favourite café, Ruby listened patiently as Fina spilled out the horrors of the previous evening. Once the memory was purged, she moved on to the details of the case.

"So we know Gasthorpe was poisoned," mused Ruby. "Do you know anything else?"

"No, unfortunately not. If it were poison – depending on what kind of poison – it might narrow down the suspects. The police seem to be operating on that assumption – that the suspects were those who were left at the end of the party: Gayatri, James, Vera, Enid, Professor Bathurst, Professor Marlston, Grace Yingxia, Jack Devenish, Pixley Hayford, and Dean Ossington," she said, pausing. "And us, of course," she continued with a grimace.

"We can rule ourselves out, at any rate," said Ruby. "But there's something I meant to ask you about the dean. I saw you talking just before the incident. You had that look on your face, the one where you're trying to act casual." She raised an interrogative eyebrow. "What was she telling you?"

Fina had forgotten all about the case of the college pilferer. Had it only been a few days ago the dean had asked them to investigate?

"It turns out she did set a trap for the thief after all, just as you suggested. Did you see that carriage clock on the mantel – the rather gaudy one?"

"I believe so. Is it valuable?"

"It is, and not only that, it's gone!"

Ruby almost dropped her teacup. "You mean to say the thief took it? Under our very noses?"

Fina nodded, agreeably conscious of having caused a sensation. "I checked the mantel before the police arrived, and it had gone. I meant to tell you but what with everything that happened it went clean out of my head."

"It's not surprising," said Ruby, "but still, I must congratulate you on your powers of observation. I don't suppose you noticed any clue as to who took it?"

"Sadly not." Fina looked at her watch. "Is there anything we can do in the meantime? I need something to keep me distracted and focused on solving this case. Because I have a feeling the police are going to return to me as a suspect very soon."

"I have the perfect distraction, Feens. Let's go to the train station."

"WENDELL!" squeaked Ruby with a mixture of relief and delight. After the train had screeched to a halt, Wendell emerged from the heavy fog encircling the train.

She rushed toward the tall figure in burgundy tweed and squeezed him uninhibitedly.

"Well, this isn't quite the welcome I expected," he said, drily. "I thought you'd be pleased to see me."

Ruby gave him a gentle, playful nudge in the ribs.

Wendell set down his suitcase and gave Fina a hug, even though she had already stretched out her hand.

"Delightful to see you again, Fina. And it is also delightful to be out of London for a while. I've been looking forward to a few days playing tourist. Perhaps we can take a boat out on the Cherwell?"

His eyes moved from Fina to Ruby and back again. "But I see you two have something else on your minds. What have the trouble-making duo been up to this time?" he queried with a grin.

The light atmosphere evaporated, much like the fog had with the departing train.

"Oh, Wendell," said Ruby, burying her face in his jacket. It was gratifying to see Ruby with Wendell – she was almost a different person when they were together. Must have been how they were as children, thought Fina with a pang of sudden jealously. She missed Connor.

"What is the matter?" he asked, looking down at Ruby and then across to Fina.

Fina said, "No one has died – at least not anyone you know. We're not in danger, not yet. At least," she added, pausing, "Ruby's not."

Wendell blinked. "What do you mean, 'at least not anyone you know'?" His voice had gone down an octave.

While Ruby stayed in her upright foetal position on Wendell's shoulder, Fina did her best – which she was sure was not enough – to explain the past twenty-four hours.

Wendell's square jaw was clenched, just like Ruby's. He took off his fashionable bowler and then put it back on again. As he lifted his arm to remove the hat, a handkerchief with a blue border peeked out of his sleeve.

"You say the police want to question you again?"

"Yes, this afternoon, after we have another appointment – we have a dress-fitting."

"Surely something as frivolous as a dress-fitting can wait at a time like this," said Wendell.

Ruby glared at him and said, "No, it's not frivolous. Besides taking our mind off things, we'll have a chance to question our client. She was at the party where the murder occurred."

"I don't think I ought to let you two go to the police alone," he said.

A wan smile spread across Ruby's face. "Ever the good brother, Wendy. But you know it's better if you avoid them as much as possible."

"You can say that again," said Wendell with a sigh. But then he stood up taller as if he had just remembered an important point. "I have a secret weapon to deal with them," he said with a wink.

"Really? Do tell," said Ruby, smoothing her hair.

Wendell tapped the side of his nose in a rather theatrical manner. "It's a surprise, but I guarantee – as much as one ever can – it will work its charms on the coppers."

With a sigh of mock exasperation, Ruby said, "Be careful, Wendy. I'm too big a cat to let a kitten fool me." Then she looked as if she regretted her older sibling statement. Fina thought it odd so many people mistook Wendell for the older sibling. They often misjudged his age. Ruby didn't necessarily look older, but she certainly acted that way. "I hope it's everything it's cracked up to be."

Sensing it might be a good time to intervene, Fina said, "The police are in college anyway, so we won't need to go to the station. It will make the whole process less of an ordeal."

Wendell nodded. "I say," he said with a start. "I've just remembered – where's Pixley?"

"He's with the police right now, answering questions," said Fina. "Otherwise he would have been here to meet you at the station."

Wendell's face scrunched up with worry. He scooped up his suitcase and put on his overcoat. The temperature had dropped to a bone-aching chill the night before.

Patting her brother's shoulder, Ruby said, "I'll leave a note with one of the scouts to tell Pixley you've arrived – with directions to your lodging at the Peacock and Parrot. Then you two can catch up. Pixley can tell you what he knows."

"And we can have a fitting with Vera-bloody-Viper-Sapperton," muttered Fina.

16

"It makes me look like a roly-poly," said Vera, running her hand over her non-existent curves.

"More like a stick insect," muttered Fina between the pins she held in her mouth. She had given herself permission to be as catty as she wanted to be today. Sitting on the floor, she was busy adjusting Vera's floor-length ball gown with caplet sleeves. Fina grudgingly admitted that the plum colour Vera had selected was spectacular.

"What was that, Fina?" said Vera in a sweet, sticky voice which held the definite edge of her namesake, a viper.

"Nothing, Vera," replied Fina, sticking in her last pin and pulling back her lips in her best impression of a braying donkey.

"I mean," said Vera, turning to Ruby who stood with her appraising pose, "it's got absolutely no SA, no SA at all."

"Would you like us to refit the bodice so you can have more cleavage?" enquired Ruby with an entirely serious look on her face.

Fina snorted.

"What was that, Fina?" asked Vera. Really, the woman was a parrot. How did they ever let her into this university? Ah yes, remembered Fina. Money and the gentry. Fina's family was technically part of the gentry, too, but her utter lack of funds made her even more bitter when someone like Vera flaunted her status.

"Mmm," was all Fina said. The fresh set of pins in her mouth gave her an excuse not to provide a real reply. She stood, but then stooped over, trying to fix one of the small beaded details. The action made her feel a little woozy so she sat back on her haunches and stared around the room. Vera was not only messy, she was a pack rat. Clothes were strewn everywhere, and bags of useless-looking items covered the surfaces of tables. Fina began to feel a little claustrophobic.

"Do you mind if I open the window?" asked Ruby. Vera nodded. The cold, fresh air revived Fina.

"I have something else you might like," said Ruby, riffling through her dress bag. She pulled out a Copen blue satin gown. The generous trumpet sleeves draped gracefully. Ruby twirled it around, revealing a dramatic décolleté back. Vera gasped. "Oh, it's lovely. I cannot wait to try it on."

Vera rushed at Ruby to take the dress. This caused Fina to tumble over to the side.

"Sorry," Vera said, perfunctorily. Fina glared at her but Vera had eyes only for the dress. She brushed her hand across the fabric.

"Fina did the beading," said Ruby with a note of pride in her voice.

Ignoring this comment, Vera glided behind the screen with the new dress.

Fina and Ruby began to make hand gestures as Vera changed. It was agreed Ruby would ask some questions.

"Ta-da!" said Vera, flouncing out in her new gown. Fina had to admit she was stunning. Now was a perfect opportunity to pop a question.

"You look stupendous," gushed Ruby in that special way she saved for difficult clients.

"Plenty of SA in this dress," said Vera, surveying herself in the mirror.

"As you say, plenty of SA," said Ruby. She gave a little cough. "Let's hope the next soirée you wear it to will be more pleasant than the last one. I say, Vera, now that we have found you *the* gown, would you mind sharing any theories about what happened last night?"

Not taking her eyes off her own figure, Vera replied, "I know everyone says it was poison, but it must have been a heart attack. Or some type of shock," she said, waving her hand with a dismissive gesture. "He didn't look healthy, and I'm sure his work must have caused a great deal of strain."

"Did you observe anything odd last night, before he died?" Fina enquired casually.

"No, darling. Nothing odd."

Fina was about to stab one of the pins into Vera's flesh, but Ruby came to the rescue. "Well, I assume you already told the police everything you know – which is nothing."

"That's right. The policeman was a real brute. But his side-kick, the detective sergeant, was good-looking." She sighed languidly, as if there were too many fish in the sea. Then she sauntered over to the settee and cleared away some detritus before reclining in a pose one might see in a women's magazine.

"I was mostly with Bathy the entire time. We had plenty to discuss," she said, lighting a cigarette. She blew smoke in Fina's direction. Fina waved it away with irritation.

"Bathy?" asked Fina incredulously. "You must be quite close."

"Well, he does take a particular ... interest in me," Vera said with a rather smug chuckle.

17

As they stood at the arched entrance to Tiscott Hall, Ruby summed up their encounter with Vera. "Despite the fact she is quite possibly the most vapid and irritating creature on the planet, I don't think she was hiding anything about the murder. She's too self-absorbed to observe anything of interest."

"Yes, a complete and utter narcissist. It seems Professor Bathurst has those tendencies as well. I wonder how they get on," said Fina.

"I've pondered that as well. Narcissists must only be a problem in a relationship when they're with someone who is *not* a narcissist, right?"

"Perhaps. Though it seems like it must go sour at some point." Fina paused. "But back to the murder. You said you don't think Vera is hiding anything about *the murder*. Do you think she's hiding something else?"

Ruby tapped her teeth. "I'm not certain, but there is something in the back of my mind. I'm sure it will come to me after I sleep on it," she said, smiling.

Fina nodded. "Sleep! What a fine idea. I could use a nap about now." She looked down at her watch. "My, we must fly!

We're supposed to meet the police at four o'clock at Fidlow Hall."

They dashed across the quad and into the cavernous Fidlow. This was Fina's least favourite building, made of large blocks of grey stone. The halls were dimly lit and, despite being at the heart of the college, no one ever seemed to be about. As if students and faculty were on a curfew. And it was always chilly.

"Ladies," said a voice behind them. It was Dean Ossington, looking a little worse for wear. She wore a high-neck burgundy lace dress, but she was missing her pearls. Her hair was askew. Fina had never thought of the dean as frail, but today she looked like a child's doll who had been loved for many years.

"I've been answering Chief Inspector Hogston's questions," she said, sighing. Her arms and shoulders relaxed, as if it had just dawned on her that the ordeal was over.

"We're on our way to answer more questions," said Fina. "Dean Ossington, I have to ask if you mentioned the college pilferer to the police," she said, lowering her voice.

"What college pilferer?" she said, smiling.

"Well, that's a relief," said Ruby. "I was wondering the same thing. If they get wind of our involvement, it's going to look even worse for us."

"My lips are sealed," said the dean, gently patting Ruby on the arm. "Did you two notice what happened with the trap I set during the party?"

Ruby and Fina nodded in unison.

"Fina told me you decided to go ahead with the plan to ensnare the thief. It was the carriage clock, wasn't it?" said Ruby, glancing at Fina for confirmation. "And it disappeared shortly after Gasthorpe died."

The dean's mouth was set in a grim line. "Yes," she said. "Our friend must have used the commotion to his advantage. But it all seems rather insignificant after what has happened," she said with a dismissive hand gesture.

Fina wasn't so sure.

As the dean prepared to depart, she said, "The police have ordered all outsiders to stay in college until further notice. I know it's hardly a festive occasion, but I've decided the best thing to do, as hostess of that ill-fated party, is to invite everyone for dinner in my rooms tonight. Can you be there at seven o'clock?"

"Surely you don't mean *everyone* at the sherry party, do you?" asked Fina.

"No. Only those who were there when Gasthorpe died. That would be the two of you, myself, Gayatri Badarur, James Matua, Vera Sapperton, Enid Wiverton, Professor Bathurst, Professor Marlston, Grace Yingxia, Jack Devenish, and Pixley Hayford."

She cocked her head to one side. "And Beatrice, of course. She will be helping me with preparations and serving."

"Would you mind if I invite my brother, Wendell? He arrived today and I promised to have dinner with him," enquired Ruby.

"Of course, Miss Dove. He's quite welcome."

"Do you think everyone will attend?" asked Fina.

The dean shrugged. "I assume so. It would be highly suspicious if they declined the invitation," she said with a twinkle in her eye.

18

Ruby and Fina entered a small, cramped room at the end of one hallway. It seemed to be more of a closet – certainly out of keeping with the beautiful airy rooms of the rest of building. It was sweltering inside. Fina sniffed and wrinkled her nose in distaste. It certainly smelled like many nervous people had been in this room today.

Hogston told them they were to be interviewed together. Fina was relieved in some ways, but might the police use it to their advantage? She knew quite well they cultivated an apparently haphazard approach to interviews in order to corner their quarry.

Whistling again, Snorscomb directed them to sit in a pair of hard chairs. Really, most uncomfortable. But she supposed that was the point.

"Ah, Detective Sergeant," said Hogston, drawing his fingers across his mouth in a zipping gesture.

"Right, sir. Sorry sir," Snorscomb replied.

Hogston leaned back in his chair, surveying the pair across the table. A small stub of a cigarette hung out of his mouth, adding to the rather dishevelled look of a man who hadn't had time for personal hygiene since the murder occurred. Cups and saucers littered the windowsill like a pile of shells on the seashore. The seashore. Home. Fina inhaled deeply, recalling the smell and the sounds of her home on the coast.

"Thank you for coming, Miss Aubrey-Havelock and Miss Dove," said the chief inspector as he stubbed out his cigarette in an ashtray which looked like the remains of a fireplace. "We have a few more questions for you, especially in light of our continued investigation."

"I'm sure we'd be delighted to help in any way we are able, Chief Inspector," said Ruby.

"That's fine, Miss Dove. Now, we are awaiting the results of the autopsy but, as I told you last night, it does look likely the cause of death was poison."

Fina let out an audible sigh of relief. Hogston turned toward her. "Yes, Miss Aubrey-Havelock. You ought to be relieved he didn't apparently die of delayed brain trauma caused either by your punch or his fall to the floor. Unless, of course, both happened. But we won't know for sure for a few more hours."

"I see," said Ruby. "So you think he was poisoned by something he ate or drank?"

"It's certainly possible, but we couldn't find anything in the drinks glasses, although we've sent them all to be analysed. As for the food, well, we won't know about that until we have the full autopsy report. We're working on the assumption it is likely that was the method of ingestion."

He cleared his throat. Snorscomb was massaging his writing hand. He must have quite a cramp by now.

"Please understand this next question is routine procedure. We are asking everyone who was present to take a look at Gasthorpe's personal belongings, to see if anything seems significant."

Hogston bent over to retrieve something from underneath

the desk. He emerged with a tray of items – almost like a jewellery shop owner – to show to the pair.

"Now," he said. "These are the items found on his person. We have a separate tray for his personal belongings that were near him."

The silver tray held a gold pocket watch, a pair of reading glasses, a tin of tobacco, a pipe, a box of mints, a tiny pencil, a small leather-bound notebook, eye-drops, a box of matches, and a woman's brassiere.

Fina could feel her eyebrows disappear into the fringe on her forehead.

"Quite right, Miss Aubrey-Havelock," said Hogston who was staring at her intently. "Does this garment belong to either of you?"

"Chief Inspector!" said Ruby in her best impression of shock and horror. "Really!"

Hogston's face remained impassive. "This is a murder enquiry, Miss Dove, so we must ask these rather indelicate questions."

"These were found on him, not in a separate coat?" Fina suggested, while Ruby played her look of shock for all it was worth.

"Good question, Miss Aubrey-Havelock. The watch, reading glasses, pipe and tobacco were all found on his person. The other items were found in the pockets of his overcoat."

"Good Lord," whispered Fina.

"Indeed, Miss Aubrey-Havelock," he said, lighting another cigarette. This, too, was a pre-smoked stub. Times must be hard in the police force, she thought absently. "Now, neither of you have any idea why he had this item of clothing in his coat?"

They shook their heads.

"It's scandalous, Chief Inspector. After all, this is a

respectable women's college," said Ruby. Fina almost broke out in a fit of giggles.

Ruby peered closer at the tray. "Are any of the boxes empty?"

"The box of matches and tobacco tin are empty ... Anything strike you as odd or out of place?"

The pair shook their heads again in unison.

It was Snorscomb's turn to reveal the next tray of items. "Here are the items found in his briefcase."

The tray was empty.

"Is this a joke?" asked Fina. Ruby shot her a sideways glance of warning.

"No, miss. We wanted to see what your reaction was. We do find it odd his briefcase was empty. At the very least his notes for his speech should be in the briefcase, but there was nothing."

"Sorry, Chief Inspector," said Ruby. "I agree it is odd, but it looks as though you have a thief as well as a murderer on your hands."

"That's not all, Miss Dove," he continued, stubbing out his one-minute cigarette in the ashtray. "Jack Devenish, Mr Gasthorpe's personal secretary, informs us important papers have gone missing from his late employer's guest room in college."

"What kind of papers?" Fina queried.

"All of them, including the deceased's last will and testament."

19

Fixing her hat more tightly to her head against the gusty October wind, Fina paused at the top of the stone steps.

"I say, Ruby. That – er – bra. It must mean Gasthorpe himself was the college pilferer!"

Ruby smiled. "I admire your logic, Watson. But your deduction is flawed. Those thefts started long before Mr Gasthorpe arrived in college."

"So they did," said Fina, crestfallen. "Then why ...? Could he have been working in conjunction with the thief?"

"Or is that what someone wants us to think?" countered Ruby.

Fina sighed, and, hat firmly pinned into place, prepared to step out into the quad. But Ruby grabbed her shoulder and held her back.

"What on earth?" said Fina.

"Shhhh," said Ruby, holding a finger to her lips. She pointed around the corner archway to gesture someone was there. Lectures were in session, so the quad was deserted. Except for Tibby, lolling about in the grass. The cat lay right next to a placard warning all students to keep off the grass.

Ruby mouthed the word "listen".

They stood with their backs scraping against the brick wall. A faint whisper reached Fina's ears.

"Gracie, you know we ought to tell them about us."

"Absolutely not, Vicky. It isn't safe, sweetie."

Fina's eyes widened. Perhaps there was more than met the eye in that relationship.

She felt a tap on her shoulder.

"Miss Aubrey-Havelock, isn't it?" said Jack Devenish. He gave her a broad smile, showing off spectacular teeth. He put out a hand to her as if they were ready to close a deal of some sort.

"Yes," said Fina, craning her head to peer up at him. The three of them looked like they were waiting in a queue for a popular event. "Hello, Mr Devenish. I meant to tell you I'm sorry for your loss."

"Hardly a loss, if you want the honest truth. I hadn't been with Gasthorpe more than a few months. And he wasn't an easy man in the best of times.' He paused. "Say, why are the three of us lined up like this?" he said, gesturing toward the front of the line where Ruby was standing.

"Ah – we – were enjoying a few minutes of sun."

"Must have been mighty quick since it's been cloudy all day."

"Yes, there was a momentary parting of the clouds," she said while she gently tapped Ruby's shoulder. Ruby turned around and smiled. "Mr Devenish," she said, giving a little bow of her head.

Fina broke the awkward silence. "Why did you become his secretary? And more to the point, why did you stay on after you found out how hard he was?"

"My, you don't waste time, do you?" he said with another dazzling smile. "Though I do admire someone who can come right to the point." He pulled out his cigarette case and offered the contents to Ruby and Fina. "Well, my last job ended up in

Scotland. I was working for a duke – he was a hard man, too. A friend let me know Gasthorpe was looking for a new secretary. Apparently, he went through one every six months, either because he fired them or they couldn't stick it."

He took a long drag on his cigarette and looked up at the pendulous clouds. "I thought I would be up for a challenge. I treat curmudgeons like Gasthorpe as a personal challenge. And I won't say the money didn't help sweeten the deal."

"The police said some papers have gone missing. Do you know if they were important – besides the will?" asked Ruby.

Jack blew a smoke ring toward the sky. He looked completely relaxed. "Yep. All of his papers. Three goddamn boxes of them. They were in his room yesterday, before the lecture, and I never went in there again till this morning. That's when I realised they'd vanished," he said, flicking his cigarette ash to the ground. "I know a lot of people who would have liked to get their hands on them. He was a journalist, which means he had a whole lot of dirt on a whole lot of people. I told the police, but it seemed to make them even more frustrated."

"Anyone in particular?" asked Fina.

"Nice try, Miss Aubrey-Havelock," he smiled.

Fina changed tack. "And what made you travel from the United States to England?"

"It's that obvious, is it?" he said, stubbing out his cigarette with his shoe. "I thought I had lost some of the accent. I've been here for what, ten years now? Came over with my mother who was born here, after my pa died."

Fina's next question was pre-empted as he looked down at his watch. "My, I'll be late if I don't leave now. I have an appointment with Professor Bathurst. We're supposed to meet in his lab at four o'clock. Could you point me in the right direction?"

Ruby sent him through the archway. Fina watched as he walked away. She hadn't noticed his slight limp before.

Ruby turned to Fina. "That's odd."

"What's odd? That he's an American?" asked Fina.

"Well, yes, that too. But what's more odd is Professor Bathurst announced this morning he'd be in town all day, attending to various errands – if the police should need him." Ruby tapped her teeth. "I wonder which one of them is lying." She glanced at her watch. "It's only four now. We don't need to dress for dinner until half-six. Let's follow Devenish to see what he's up to."

"Really?" squeaked Fina. She was used to sleuthing in unfamiliar places but not in college.

"Really. Follow me to the chemistry laboratory!" Ruby said, dashing off from the archway into the next quad.

She stopped in front of the building so quickly Fina almost tumbled into her.

"Let's sneak around the back. Remember? There's a great big bank of windows into the laboratory. Maybe we can see who is in there."

Treading carefully, they sidled up to the windows overlooking a long, narrow room. Fina peered in at the variously coloured test tubes scattered about like magicians' potions. At first, she couldn't see any movement inside. Then her eyes adjusted to the gloom – no lights were on inside the lab.

In the far corner of the long room, she could make out two figures. They looked like they were arguing. They moved a little closer toward the window.

Ruby whispered, "I cannot see who is moving in there."

"It's Vera and Jack!" breathed Fina.

Ruby looked at Fina as if she were joking.

"It looks like they're arguing about something. Now Vera is leaving."

The door slammed. Jack shrugged. He began to move about the laboratory, slowly and methodically.

"Now it looks like he's searching the laboratory. Do you think he's looking for the papers?"

"Maybe. But it doesn't look like he's found anything. He looks quite angry about it, too."

Fina winced as she straightened her legs. "Look, he's off, too. Let's go. I'm stiff."

"Wait. See who walked in."

Fina looked through one of the panes which had been replaced and therefore was crystal clear. "What the devil?"

"I suppose Gayatri has her reasons for being in a chemistry laboratory, unlike Mr Devenish."

"Yes, but why is she looking so furtive? She's searching as well." Fina watched as Gayatri came to a small closet in the front of the room. She unlocked it and disappeared inside. Must be larger than it looks, thought Fina. Gayatri exited a moment later with a smile of triumph on her face. She carried her bag with her so it was hard to tell if she could have found an object and stowed it away.

Fina heard a gentle step behind them, like a cat ready to pounce on its unwitting prey. She whirled around.

"James!" she said, hand over heart. "You gave me a turn!"

He smiled his usual sheepish smile. "What are you two doing?"

Fina turned to Ruby for help. Ruby said, "The laboratory room was locked and I needed to check on a few things – safety things I was worried about. So we thought to see if the windows – since they're more like French windows – were open."

If James found this to be a feeble explanation, he didn't show it.

"What are you doing here?" asked Fina.

"Oh, I was looking for Vera. Or Gayatri. I thought they might be in the laboratory."

"You're in luck. Vera just left," Ruby said, clearly not wanting to interrupt their surveillance of Gayatri. "But be forewarned, James. She didn't look to be in a terribly good mood."

20

"I have an idea," said Ruby, looking down at her watch. "We have just enough time to carry it out. I'd like to bring Wendell along, but we don't have time to fetch him."

"Where are we going?"

"To Cowley."

"Cowley? Why on earth ...?"

"Let's dash. I'll explain while we're on our way."

Soon they were aboard the bus to Cowley Road. Passing Magdalen College and the bridge over the River Cherwell, Fina reflected on how easy it was to live in the Oxford bubble – to never leave its comfortable sense of time standing still, of a place where the outside world never intruded upon its perfectly cut grounds. But she knew this was simply an illusion.

The bus came to a slow, trundling halt after a few minutes on the Cowley Road, just past the Morris automobile factory.

"Will you tell me now why we're here?" asked Fina through gritted teeth.

Ruby pointed at a line of shabby shops a few metres away from where they had exited. Fina began to relax as she breathed in the fresh air – a welcome contrast to the stuffy bus.

Without further explanation, Ruby began to walk toward the shops. Fina followed like a dutiful dog who had tired of walkies. Spink's Pawnbroker was first in line. Fina peered in at the jumble of furniture, clothes and shoes in the window. Was it open? It certainly looked dark.

Ruby pushed on the door but it was locked. They tried the next shop, this time with more success. Fina had been to a pawnbroker's just a few times in her short life. She enjoyed sorting through items, seeking a bit of treasure. But a pawn shop was an inherently sad, depressing place. A place of dreams dashed and discarded.

Fina chided herself for her rather melodramatic romantic indulgence. Must be the lack of sleep, she thought.

A small, spritely man emerged from the nether regions of the shop. Unlike his surroundings, which were grimy and cluttered, this man was immaculate. He sported a jaunty cap and red braces. His smile was the kind which could be either ironic or genuine.

Tipping his cap at Ruby and Fina, he said, "What can I do for you two ladies? May I interest you in some lovely stones that just arrived?"

"Thank you, Mr—" said Ruby.

"Call me Charlie."

"Charlie, then. We have a friend who pawned a valuable item and we're looking to buy it back for him – as a surprise."

"Well, that's uncommonly kind of you," he said, grinning cautiously. Fina wondered if he heard this line very often. "What item are you looking for?"

"A silver cow creamer. In mint condition," said Ruby.

Charlie's eyes narrowed. He sucked at his teeth. "Well, now. A young lady like yourselves came in with a cow creamer. She bargained hard with me, but I wouldn't give her what she wanted. She comes in here about once a week. It's a rare day I strike a bargain with her, mind you."

"A lady!" Fina sneaked a glance at Ruby, but her friend was studiously avoiding her gaze.

"That must be our friend's sweetheart," improvised Ruby. "Do you think she might come back today?"

"It's possible." He looked at the ancient grandfather clock partially hidden by the bits and bobs of the pawn shop. "She comes in when it begins to get dark, right around half past five. It's almost five o'clock now, but she might come early. A desperate woman if I've ever seen one."

"Could you describe her?" asked Fina.

He scratched his chin and ran his fingers up and down his braces. "Well, I can tell she's a toff of some sort, though mind you she could just be dressing that way. The main thing is she wears a net, or a what's-it?"

"Veil?" asked Ruby, hopefully.

Charlie snapped his fingers. "That's it. A veil. So I can't see her face."

"Thanks for your help, Charlie. We'll try out the other pawnshops and will be watching the shop to see if it's our friend. Would you come out and wave at us if you see her?" asked Ruby. She withdrew half a crown and slid it across the desk, which was covered in a thick layer of dust.

Charlie pushed it back. "Thanks, but no thanks, miss. Happy to help."

Ruby and Fina smiled. As they turned to go, Ruby spun around and said, "Please don't let her know we were here, Charlie. It's a surprise, you understand."

Charlie winked.

After exhausting the possibilities of the other four shops on the street, Fina began to cough from the accumulation of dust in her lungs. "Are we going to return to Charlie's? My feet are killing me," she said, looking down at her heels sadly. "I would have put on more comfortable shoes if I had known we were going on this expedition."

"We'll go back to Charlie's. There's a ledge outside a shopfront across from his shop. I think we can sit there – out of sight – and wait for our thief to arrive," said Ruby.

As they made their way in the dusk toward Charlie's, Fina mused, "So it wasn't a man after all, despite the women's underthings. Who do you think it could be? Enid? Vera? Grace?"

"It could be anyone if they dressed the part," said Ruby as she wiped away the dust on the ledge with her gloved hand.

They waited. Twilight had descended – Fina's favourite time of the day, when everything took on a luminous quality.

Click, click, click.

The sound of heels rushing across the pavement made them both sit up straight. They peered around the corner. Fina saw a figure in a green tweed suit approaching Charlie's shop. The figure wore a pillbox hat with a veil. Fina began to move, but Ruby held her back gently. She whispered, "Wait until Charlie gives us the signal."

After what seemed to be an interminable three minutes, the tweed figure exited, moving back in the direction of Oxford. Charlie rushed out of the shop, waving his hands at Ruby and Fina.

The pair dashed across the road, waving and smiling at Charlie. The tweed figure seemed to be picking up speed with each step. She turned a corner off the main road. Ruby and Fina followed close behind. Nothing and no one was in sight. They looked in the nooks and crannies of the street, but could find no sign of the thief.

A little way down the block, a figure in a nun's habit walked slowly toward them. "Look!" said Ruby. "It's the Iffley Queen of Cowley Road!"

Fina looked at her friend as if she was a bit soft in the head. "Who's that?" she whispered as the apparent nun walked toward them.

"A local character who dresses as a nun in a white or pale dress. She's a fixture here. Let's ask her about our thief."

As they approached, Fina could see there was something not quite nun-like about this person. The habit was correct, but it was worn as a costume.

"Excuse me, Iffley Queen," said Ruby. The nun halted and bestowed on them a beatific smile. "Yes, my child?"

"Did you see a woman in tweed run down this street?"

"Yes, my child," said the Iffley Queen, folding together her hands which then disappeared into her sleeves. "She was running – as best she could manage in those heels. She went in the direction of Oxford." She paused.

"Yes?" said Fina.

"It was peculiar. She ran with a carriage clock in her arms."

21

Tap, tap.

"Would you see who is at the door, Feens?" asked Ruby as she was sewing a button back onto the apricot-and-brown day dress she was wearing. Fina admired the asymmetrical line of the collar.

Fina rose and opened the door a crack. She saw the trembling curls of Beatrice before she saw anything else. Was the woman nervy or just full of energy?

"Yes, Beatrice? I'm answering the door as Ruby is busy at the moment."

Beatrice moved one errant curl from her forehead. "There are two gentlemen downstairs waiting on Miss Dove."

"Which two gentlemen?"

"One is, oh dear, I'm having trouble with names today. A Mr Hayford," she said as her head bent in the effort of remembrance.

"And the second said he was a ... Mr Dove," she said with a look of horror at her own words. "Miss Dove isn't really Mrs Dove, is she?"

Fina grinned. "No, Beatrice. He's Wendell Dove, Ruby's brother."

Beatrice looked relieved. "Well, that's all right I'm sure, miss. The two of them wanted to come upstairs, but I said it was absolutely out of the question. The idea!" she said, snorting with self-righteous indignation. "They're waiting to escort the two of you to the dean's dinner."

"Are you also coming tonight?"

Beatrice's curls quivered in assent. "She told me to. She wants everyone there who was there last night. She fancies herself a sleuth!" Now Beatrice was warming to her subject. "I've got a few ideas of my own, mind you."

"Such as?"

"Those two – the poet and the professor – Professor Marlston. Those two are thick as thieves. Up to no good if you ask me."

"What does that have to do with the murder?"

"Well, last night, during the sherry party, the two of them were like peas in a pod. Walked everywhere together. Didn't talk to another living soul. And it wasn't just that. They kept peering around, like they were looking for someone or something. Like a tiger might pop out of the potted plant!"

Fina decided to take advantage of Beatrice's loquaciousness. She knew it would take quite a while for Ruby to finish her sewing project – and she could tell her the details later. "So you say Miss Yingxia and Professor Marlston were inseparable. Couldn't the same be said of Esmond Bathurst and Vera Sapperton?"

Beatrice's eyes flickered. She licked her lips. "Yes, miss. But those two weren't looking around all the time. They only had eyes for each other, if you know what I mean," she said with a wink. Fina winked back, even though it was more of a squint.

She hadn't yet figured out how to make one eyelid close like a shutter.

"Though that poor Miss Enid Wiverton. She was hanging on, or hanging around, Miss Sapperton. If you want my tuppence-worth, the girl needs to find herself some new friends. Ones who will treat her right."

Fina nodded hurriedly, wanting to get the conversation back on track. "Did you notice anything else last night? You were the one in charge of the serving, so do you have any theories about how the poison got into the food or drink?"

Beatrice shook her head but proceeded to expound on her theories anyway. "I'm blessed if I can see how it would get into the food. There was nothing that could hold it, if you take my meaning – nothing that could soak it up. What's more, if the murderer had put it on one of the canapés on a tray, how could they be sure Mr Gasthorpe would take that very one? And if they put it on a whole tray, then other people would have been taken ill or died, too."

"Mmm ... go on."

"Well, it seems it had to be the drink. But that doesn't seem right, either. You'd have to be standing right next to him to put something in his drink, because otherwise you'd have the same problem as you'd have with the tray of food."

"Who was standing near enough to him?"

Beatrice leaned against the doorframe and bit her lip. "Well, there was Mr Devenish and Dean Ossington, of course. They were definitely the closest to him all night. If we go strictly by that, they're the most likely. But all the rest of the guests marched up and shook his hand at one time or another, seeing as how he was the guest of honour."

She pondered for a moment. "And then there's you," added Beatrice, eyes wide again at her own revelation.

"Yes, yes, Beatrice, but you know I didn't do it."

"Maybe it's the man who is waiting downstairs. The journalist. He looks shifty."

Fina sighed. "I'm sure it's not Mr Hayford. Why would he want to kill Mr Gasthorpe?"

"Jealousy?" asked Beatrice.

"Jealousy?" Fina parroted.

"Yes, since they're both journalists. And Mr Gasthorpe is – or was – a big name."

"Seems like a weak motive." Fina gave her a playful grin. "What about you, Beatrice? You certainly had the most access of anyone all night."

"Oh no, miss!" Beatrice seemed genuinely afraid.

Fina decided she'd better backtrack. "I was joking, Beatrice. Just joking..." she trailed off.

But Beatrice had disappeared.

Fina turned back to Ruby. "Have you figured out the identity of our tweed thief?"

Ruby removed a pin from her mouth. "I think so, Feens, but I need to test a few more theories before I'm sure."

22

A quivering, foggy tension filled Dean Ossington's sitting room.

The party looked jolly enough from the outside, thought Fina. The dean's sitting room was aglow from the fireplace. The mantel was adorned with fresh branches of autumn leaves. And the drinks were flowing. Everyone who had been there last night – at least at the end of the party – was present. With the exception, of course, of Mr Gasthorpe. Fina had to admit the dean was brilliant, even though she knew how dangerous it was to play sleuth from her experiences of the past year.

Everyone made polite conversation, but they were all trying a bit too hard, thought Fina. Or was her mind playing tricks on her? She tried to focus. Then she realised it wasn't the content of the conversations which seemed odd; it was the body language. Everyone, even those with naturally poised or slumped posture, was standing ramrod-straight.

A knock came at the door. Beatrice scurried over to open it. Her eyes widened.

Hogston and Snorscomb entered, tipping their hats and then removing them. "Let me take your coats, gentlemen," said Beatrice with a curtsy so exaggerated it looked like she was playing a French maid in some dreadful West End flop.

"No, no thank, you Miss Truelove," said Hogston. "We won't be here long." He put his beloved homburg back on his head. Must be his form of a security blanket, Fina thought.

Dean Ossington came up to greet them. Hogston leaned over and whispered in her ear. It was the lowest whisper Fina had ever *not* heard – utter and complete silence had descended on the room with the appearance of the police.

Snorscomb stood aside while Hogston took his place by the fireplace. He waved a folder in front of everyone.

"I apologise for interrupting your little get-together," said Hogston. "But I did want to tell you all the autopsy results."

"Really, Chief Inspector," said Victoria. "Must we?"

"We must, Miss Marlston, we must," he replied.

"That's Professor Marlston to you," she said, peering at him like a specimen.

"Yes, quite, Professor Marlston. We're still working on the internal analysis, but we can confirm Mr Gasthorpe was poisoned."

"By what, Chief Inspector?" Jack queried with a touch of belligerence.

Hogston sucked in his gut before exhaling, "Nicotine. Most likely liquid nicotine. It's difficult to detect in an autopsy, especially since Gasthorpe was a heavy smoker. But the pathologist is confident it was nicotine."

Glancing around the room, Fina could see a mixture of dumbfounded expressions: mouths hanging open and plenty of rapid blinking.

"You mean like in a cigarette?" asked Grace, quickly stubbing out her own cigarette in the tray. A twinge of disgust passed across her face.

"Precisely, Miss Yingxia," said Hogston. "The difference is

the chemical is concentrated. It's usually used for insecticides and the like."

"So any of us could have purchased it," said James, rubbing his chin.

"Yes," mused Hogston, rubbing his chin in a mirroring gesture. "But it wouldn't be that easy. And we do have to consider the fact many of you here are connected in some way with chemistry, which means you could produce your own quantity in a laboratory."

Fina was sure she could make out little beads of sweat on Professor Bathurst's forehead.

He began to stammer, a wholly unusual trait for someone who was usually so mellifluous. "I– I– I suspect you will want to check my laboratory, Chief Inspector," he said, fumbling around in his pockets. He produced a key and held it up like it was the holy grail. He walked over and bestowed it on Hogston.

"We will be checking the laboratory, of course, but we don't hold out much hope as the murderer has likely already cleaned up his or her tracks," the officer said, looking at them all, one by one, in a slow, scanning motion.

"Chief Inspector, can you tell us how Mr Gasthorpe ingested the poison?" queried Dean Ossington.

Victoria jumped in. "Could it have been his pipe? It was practically an appendage to him."

Hogston smiled, a small, crooked smile. "If you think he smoked himself to death – which would let all of you off the hook – you're wrong. It would take considerably more than that."

He held up his hands, forestalling any possible protests. "It could have been in his pipe, however. But it would still be murder. Someone would have had to put the liquid nicotine in his pipe itself or in his tin of tobacco. And, as Detective Sergeant

Snorscomb and myself now know, any of you could have put it in his tobacco tin."

"Couldn't some other guest – who left early – have slipped it in the tin? In other words, not one of us?" asked Gayatri.

"No," said Jack. "You see, I know Mr Gasthorpe didn't refill his pipe until after – after he had the altercation. And he had refilled it and smoked it before that. I know because when he fell on the floor, his pipe lost its tobacco as well."

All eyes slid toward Fina. She felt as tormented as a roasted herring.

"Yes," said Hogston. "If the tin had been tampered with prior to the altercation, he would already have been poisoned."

Wendell cleared his throat. Fina looked over at Ruby, who gave her brother a warning look – which he ignored. "Inspector," he began.

"*Chief* Inspector, sir. And who, might I ask, are you?" Hogston said, lurching toward Wendell with what Fina could only call a swaggering step. Oh dear.

"I'm Wendell Dove, Miss Dove's brother. *Lieutenant* Wendell Dove."

23

Hogston froze, mid-step. Fina had to hand it to Wendell. He certainly knew how to throw the police off-guard. Absolutely spiffing to see the look on Hogston's face. His posture changed from swagger to business-like.

"Lieutenant Dove. As in lieutenant of ...?" enquired Hogston.

"Her Majesty's Royal Navy," said Wendell, casually removing a folded letter from inside his coat pocket. He handed it over to Hogston.

Hogston's eyes scanned the letter. "Captain Marshall ... highly recommends ... attention," he mumbled to himself. The chief inspector peered at Wendell. "Right. Good to meet you," he said, sticking out his hand, much in the same way Jack Devenish had the night before. Fina was glad to see Hogston's scarlet face. Serves the blighter right, she thought.

"Do you have any thoughts on this case, Lieutenant?"

When Fina and Ruby had met up with Wendell earlier that summer in St Kitts, the first thing Fina noticed about him was the way he carried himself. When she found out he was a lieutenant in the navy, it all began to make sense. She had chided Ruby, however, for not telling her earlier.

"Not at the moment, sir, but I would like to be kept informed of any new developments," he said, looking at Hogston and Snorscomb. "If that follows your protocol, of course. I do have some past experience in military intelligence."

Ha! Thought Fina to herself. A giggle down in the depths of her stomach begin to rise. The whole situation was absurd. She snuck a peek at Ruby. Fina was surprised to see a look of, what was it? Jealousy. How odd sibling dynamics could be. Wendell was stealing her thunder. She was glad to discover a small human weakness in her friend who so often held everything together as if it were easy.

"Of course, Lieutenant Dove," said Hogston, offering Wendell a calling card that had seen better days. "Ring me up on that number if you have questions or find out anything."

Hogston backed up as if to take his leave. "Well, I wish all of you a pleasant evening ... at least as pleasant as it might be under the circumstances."

And with a pointed look at Pixley, he said, "And I expect all of you to be discreet about this matter. You especially, Mr Hayford."

Pixley's head bobbed as if it were against his own wishes.

Hogston continued to walk backward like a crab, with Snorscomb following suit, until they reached the door.

Ruby bent over and whispered to Fina. "Notice anything odd about the mantel?"

Fina looked carefully at the photos and knick-knacks and shook her head.

Then she saw it. The carriage clock which had gone missing the night before.

"Well, well," murmured Fina. "Let's make a beeline for Ossie before we sit down to dinner."

The pair marched over to Ossington, who had been giving directions to Beatrice for the final place settings.

"Dean Ossington, have you noticed the bait you set out last night has reappeared on your mantel this evening?"

Ossington craned her neck. Her eyes bulged. She fairly sputtered, something she never did. "But – but how did it get there? I'll swear it wasn't there before everyone arrived."

"It seems our thief has had a fit of remorse," said Ruby. "Perhaps she or he is afraid the police will search all of our rooms. The thief has no way of knowing who knows about the thefts in college, so I imagine she or he will be anxious to avoid any possible association with the murder."

"Wait a moment." Fina blinked as she felt one of the few certain facts in this case slipping away from her grasp. "I thought we were certain the culprit was female?"

"Not entirely," answered Ruby. "Anyone can put on a dress and heels. A slight man with a tenor voice could easily put us off the scent by masquerading as a woman."

The dean, two steps behind in the conversation, was still gazing at the fireplace. "But how did the thief manage to slip it onto the mantel unnoticed?"

"I have a theory about that. This person is clearly a good thief in the sense she or he generally gets away with taking things without people noticing," said Ruby in a low voice.

"Yes, but you cannot carry a carriage clock behind your back and hope no one notices," said Fina.

Ruby moved her head to the side. "I agree. The only way it would be possible is with a bag."

"Well, that would be all the women, wouldn't it?" asked the dean.

"No, not necessarily. Some of the men might have had briefcases or schoolbags, and likewise some of the women might have only had clutches."

The dean paused, twisting her pearls at her neck. "Let me confer with Beatrice to make sure my memory is correct," she said, rushing over to the scout, who was preparing a tray in the corner.

She returned and declared, "Mr Matua, Miss Yingxia, Miss Wiverton, and Miss Sapperton all had bags of some sort. At least, ones they carried about for a little while before depositing them with Beatrice."

"So that leaves out Gayatri, plus Professors Marlston and Bathurst," said Fina. "Though it seems unlikely it would be Bathurst in any case since he has limited access to the college."

The dean nodded her confirmation. Then she gave a little sigh of satisfaction. "At least we know one of them must be the college thief! Well done."

Ruby said, a little wistfully, "I wish it were as easy to narrow down the murder suspects."

24

At dinner, Fina sat next to Grace on her left and Enid on her right. She was quite pleased about this because she hadn't had a chance to talk to either of them about the murder. The room was rather cosy, with a few mismatched chairs and tablecloths. Ruby sat across from her, next to Victoria and James. The first course, a delectable consommé, warmed Fina's belly. She felt more sociable and amiable now.

She turned to Grace in between spoonfuls of soup. Fina tried very hard not to spatter any on her own mauve dress, let alone on Grace's tangerine crepe trouser-suit.

"I am glad we have a chance to get acquainted," said Fina. "I'm keen on your new volume, *Go Lightly*." Fina thought it was progress she didn't feel bad about this slight lie. She had read it, but she had read it this morning. Fortunately, it was poetry, so one could skim it quite quickly. Though she knew that wasn't the point.

Grace's face lit up. "How splendid! What did you enjoy about it?"

Fina gulped. "Oh, I'm afraid I'm not one for poetry in general – I enjoy it, but I'm frightfully dense when it comes to the greater meaning. The poem about sailors working on the docks was delightful ... where was it? I ask because I know the city was important."

"Liverpool. That's the title of the poem," sighed Grace wistfully. "That's where I grew up, you see. My father worked on the docks and my mother ran a small newsstand near the docks. That's how they met. Though they were both born in Liverpool, my mother's parents were Chinese. My grandfather was a Chinese sailor who came to work in the port and never left because he met my grandmother."

"Well, I've been to those docks myself, and I felt like you captured the senses so well – particularly the smell," said Fina, wrinkling her nose.

Grace chuckled. "Yes, it does take some getting used to. I suppose I like it because it brings back fond memories. Plenty of characters roamed those docks. Saltier than saltwater, some of them."

"Are you going back to Liverpool at the end of your fellowship here?"

Grace's spoon clattered into the fortunately empty bowl of soup. Everyone paused and turned to stare at her. She gave them all a reassuring smile and they went back to their conversations. Fina noticed Victoria gave her a rather sharp look.

Grace dabbed the corners of her mouth. "I'm not sure where I'll be going, but after the goings-on here, I might be leaving sooner rather than later."

"You mean the murder?"

"Yes, that too, of course. But, well, there's an atmosphere here. And..." She paused and lowered her voice. "There's something else. A matter of trust."

"Has someone let you down? That's a shame."

"No. At least, not in the way you mean. But yes, I do feel let down, and a bit frightened. You see, I don't know who did it, or why, but ... some of my poems have been stolen."

Fina's eyes widened. "You mean they've been published under another name? Aren't there legal processes to address that? Or at least university policies?"

Grace pursed her lips together in a grim line. "I wish it were as simple as that, because at least I would still know where they were. You see, someone has been stealing my poems – literally snatching them out of my room!"

She let out a great whooshing sigh. "It feels good to tell someone else about it. I've only told Professor Marlston."

Fina's mind raced. Should she tell her about the other patterns of theft? Perhaps this was a ruse to get her to talk about it?

"I'm so sorry to hear that. You ought to know you're not the only one to have had things pilfered in college."

Grace's eyebrows shot upward. Fina noticed her left eyelid began to twitch, ever so slightly.

"You might tell the dean," whispered Fina. "By the way, did the thief take anything else?"

"Such as?"

"Necklaces, rings – or perhaps some rather private garments?"

Once again, Grace's eyebrows lifted, this time disappearing into her fringe. "How did you know that?" she whispered, with wide-eyed admiration.

Fina felt aglow with her apparently superior sleuthing skills. Getting a bit carried away, she replied, "I have my sources."

"I see," said Grace, absently flipping her fork over and over again on the tablecloth. "And what kind of sources might they be?" she asked with a slow smile.

Fina was saved from responding by the arrival of the main course, a delicious-looking roast beef with Yorkshire pudding.

Everyone tucked in with gusto. Fina had plenty of experience with sleuthing now, and knew how hungry it made her. Well, she was always hungry – but more hungry than usual.

She looked across at Ruby, who was in a rather intense conversation with Victoria. The professor was folding and refolding her napkin into a small square.

As everyone was coming to the end of the main course it seemed like a good time to observe each guest. James looked delighted he was sitting next to Gayatri. He jabbered away about something, while Gayatri looked on at him fondly – as one might do with an overexcited younger sibling. Dean Ossington engaged in sporadic, staccato bits of conversation with Jack. That looked like hard going, but they both seemed to be making an effort. Pixley and Wendell were next. They looked completely unaffected by the atmosphere and were engaged in good-natured ribbing of one another. Esmond and Vera were locked in intense conversation, as usual. The difference this time was in the intonation and agitated hand gestures. They looked worried and somewhat upset with each other. A lovers' tiff?

And then, completing the circle, was Enid. Fina had noticed Enid trying to make conversation with Vera, but that was simply an impossible task when Esmond was in the picture. Enid pushed the peas around on her plate, making hypnotic patterns and blobs.

Fina leaned over in an exaggerated way to pull Enid out of her reverie. "I'm not much of a fan of peas, either," she said as her opening, rather pathetic, gambit. "Though I must say these taste like they must be fresh from the college garden."

"I'm sorry, what?" enquired Enid, gazing at her blankly. The girl was still hunched over as if she had been told she was taking up too much space at the table. Fina recognised that look because she often felt that way too. A rush of sympathy for Enid overtook her.

"How have you been handling the dreadful news – not to mention what happened last night?"

Enid shrugged, as if murder was an everyday occurrence in her life. "It was dreadful, but I've been getting on with it today."

"Any theories about what happened?" asked Fina in a whisper.

"Not really. I was near Vera all night. I did watch most people, though. I do that often..." She trailed off.

Well, this was going to be like pushing a boulder up a mountain. Fina tried a different tack.

"You were with Vera most of the night. Did you two talk? You must have had a great deal to chatter about if you were with her all night."

Instead of rearranging her peas, Enid began to smash them with the back of her fork. Soon she had a green patty of peas at the centre of her plate.

"Well, you know, she was quite busy. She's a very popular girl, you know."

"Of course she is," said Fina, literally biting her tongue so she didn't add a sarcastic line to the end of her sentence. Why in heaven's name did this girl worship Vera?

"But I will say she's been different lately."

Little goose-pimples popped up on Fina's arm. "Oh, how so?" she said with forced casualness.

Enid set down her fork and looked up at the ceiling. "It's a good question. I'm not sure. She's always been quite a bubbly, enthusiastic person. She's been that more frequently. But lately, I think she's also had more bouts of bad temper."

"And I take it this isn't a monthly occurrence," said Fina drily.

"Oh no," said Enid with a voice which indicated she missed Fina's intended meaning. "I mean, one day she's sparkling and the next day, well, it pains me to say this ... but she's been quite spiteful."

"No!" said Fina as dramatically as she could muster. It was rather loud, though, because both Ruby and Gayatri looked over at her, enquiringly.

Enid was warming to her subject. "Yes. The other day she said to me, 'Enid, you are absolutely forgettable.' And I suppose I am. I grew up in a village near Wolverhampton where everyone kept to themselves. My mother said it was always best to keep your head down and work. That was the best way – don't stand out too much, she always said."

Fina grabbed Enid's arm. That Vera was a nasty piece of work. "Enid, you are absolutely memorable. I know Vera must have said it because she was feeling bad about herself – not about you."

For the first time that evening, Fina saw Enid smile. "You think so?"

"Yes. And another thing," said Fina. "You might find it healthy to stay away from Vera for a while. I have a feeling her moodiness is only going to worsen."

"Pssst. Feens," said Ruby, waving her into the small hallway of the dean's rooms, stuffed with coats. "I want to watch Vera. And maybe Enid, too. Can you stand going out tonight – to a club in the wicked metropolis? We'll be out quite late!"

Fina had already thought longingly of her bed. She sighed. "Yes, of course. If you think it will help. Do you think one of them is the thief?"

"It's possible. But I have other reasons as well."

In the silence which fell between them, Fina surmised that was all she was going to find out from Ruby.

There was a sudden rush of heels clacking on the linoleum and Fina's ears burned as Vera stepped into the hallway. "What are you two whispering about?"

Ruby turned and bestowed her best false smile on Vera and Enid tiptoed in behind her. "We were just discussing going to a club later tonight – in London."

"Sounds like a marvellous idea," squealed Vera with delight.

"How will you be let back into college?" asked Enid with genuine concern.

Ruby tossed her blue handkerchief at Enid in a playful dismissive gesture. "You either bribe one of the scouts before you leave. Or you just stay out all night and arrive in the morning!"

Enid's mouth dropped open.

"What's this?" asked Gayatri, joining the growing crowd in the hallway.

"We're going to London – to a club. Would you like to join us?" asked Fina, realising too late she wasn't sure if others were supposed to tag along on their adventure.

Gayatri frowned. "But Fina, you know the likes of Ruby and myself won't be admitted to a London club."

Ruby laid a gentle hand on Gayatri's shoulder. "Yes, but we'll be going to the White Rabbit. Wendell told me about it," she said, nodding toward Wendell who had joined the crowd and was now squeezed between the doorframe and Gayatri.

He nodded. "Yes, I know the owner. We won't have any problems there. Good music, too."

"Well, that's settled," said Vera in a satisfied voice. "Who's in?"

Like children in a classroom, they began to raise their hands. Enid was the last one to give in to peer pressure. Pixley wandered in and raised his hand with a mischievous smile. Cheeky. He didn't even know what he was agreeing to.

"I say," said a voice from behind Wendell. A head with floppy hair popped up over his shoulder. "Am I invited, too?"

Gayatri sighed. "Of course you are, James."

"Right," said Ruby. "Everyone meet at the station at eleven o'clock."

25

Smoke rings floated up to the low-hanging, half-timbered ceiling.

Fina settled her back into the corner of the wooden booth of the pub, watching Pixley's smoke rings beginning to form a small cloud above his head. They had agreed to review what they knew about the murder before they boarded the train for their nocturnal adventure. Fina was self-conscious about wearing her slinky silver gown in a pub so she pulled her coat tighter around her, despite the stifling warmth emanating from the fireplace.

She dabbed her brow with the green handkerchief Ruby had made especially for her. "Well, I'm glad that's over," she said, taking a long sip of her cider.

"Yes, it was rather unbearable in general," agreed Pixley, tapping his cigarette in a glass ashtray. "But Wendell and I had a grand old time together."

"I haven't had a chance to ask you about your theories as to what happened last night."

He shrugged and brushed a speck of invisible lint off of his impeccable light grey suit. "I spent most of the evening with our circle of friends in the corner, as you know."

"Did you go out at any time, or notice anyone tampering with the coats on the coat stand?"

He shook his head sadly. "It does strike me anyone could have tampered with the tin of tobacco. All they would have had to do is take the tin from the pocket on the way out, fix up the mixture in the bathroom and then return the tin to the jacket on the way back. It would have been quite easy – and unlikely anyone would take notice."

"I did spot that you were absent some time before I had my, er, interaction with Gasthorpe," said Fina, almost daring him to lie.

Pixley shifted in his seat. "Yes, I was gone for a while. The party was stuffy – in both senses of the word. I felt like I needed to work the old lungs a bit outside."

Ruby and Wendell appeared, drinks in hand.

"What are you two chatting about so intently?" asked Wendell.

"Oh, just the murder," said Pixley.

"The four of us haven't had a chance to talk about it. What do you say we write out what we know about the suspects? There are quite a few," said Wendell, pulling a notebook and pencil out of his worn but lovely leather bag.

This habit of writing down suspects was apparently a family trait. Ruby looked slightly put out that it wasn't her suggestion. Or was she showing caution in front of Pixley? Surely they could trust him?

Whatever hesitations she might have had suddenly vanished with the first sip of her cider.

"I'm game. Who is our first suspect?"

Pixley piped up. "That Devenish character – the secretary. I don't trust Americans and he seems like a rather devious character if ever I've seen one. And why couldn't he do his job and look after those papers of Gasthorpe's?" His fist banged on the table in frustration. "I tried to ask him a few questions about what might have happened to them, and he said, 'No comment'."

Fina was sure Pixley would have asked more than a few questions.

Ruby grinned. "I agree he strikes one as a little too polished – and yet not polished."

"And he's only been Gasthorpe's secretary for a few months. He could have taken the job to get information or to murder Gasthorpe," said Fina.

Wendell scribbled furiously. He looked up. "Why? What does he gain by his death?"

Pixley said, "Well, there is that missing will. I don't know what he'd have to gain from destroying it – it's not like Gasthorpe's estate would go to Devenish if he died intestate."

"Good point," said Ruby. "Do we know what was in the will? I know he was unmarried, with no children."

They all shook their heads. Fina pondered writing to her solicitor, Mr Tufton. She decided she would. But it wouldn't get her very far with the problem they had now.

"Well, going back to Devenish, I cannot see he had any motive to kill him, unless it was some sort of personal revenge," said Ruby. Everyone nodded agreement.

"Right," said Wendell. "I'll put down a question mark as to his motive. But he had one of the strongest opportunities to have committed the crime – he knew Gasthorpe's habits and was with him the entire night."

"It strikes me that makes him even less of a suspect," said Fina, "Because he would be the most likely suspect."

With a flourish, Wendell made a point in his notebook. "Next we have Professor Bathurst."

"Well, we did see..." Fina trailed off, looking at Ruby for confirmation before continuing. "We heard from Devenish they were supposed to meet up this afternoon, but Bathurst said he was going to town to do some errands."

"And that reminds me," said Ruby. "We saw—" she cleared her throat, "I ought to say we *watched* Devenish search Bathurst's laboratory this afternoon."

Wendell made a quick note in the Devenish column.

"So it's possible Bathurst was lying, and that he did meet Devenish somewhere else, or he was truthful and was in town all day."

Pixley waved a hand as if he were asking to be called on during a seminar. "I did see Bathurst this morning, when I was walking to meet Wendell. He was on the other side of the street, heading into town." He paused. "I must admit my journalistic tendencies shifted into gear. I followed him a bit, just because I was intrigued to see where he was going."

"What would he gain from Gasthorpe's murder?"

Pixley waved his hand again. "We're forgetting Gasthorpe was a journalist. Now, in my experience, someone like that doesn't get to the top of his profession – not to mention earning himself a great deal of money despite his supposedly hard-scrabble beginnings – without a little, shall we say, ethical bending of professional standards?"

"I'm trying to weave my way through that rather vague statement, but I'm afraid I'm getting lost, Pixley. Could you try again?"

"All I mean is journalists – if they choose to go down this path, mind you – are in an excellent position to set up a little extortion business on the side. After all, Gasthorpe collected all kinds of life stories, remember?"

"And the papers in his room and briefcase all went missing at around the same time. Scarcely a coincidence," said Wendell.

"The will might have been taken with all the papers and the thief might not have even known what the contents of the papers might be. If I were worried about a scandal, I would simply take all of his papers."

Ruby gave a slow nod. "Yes ... it does seem like that is a particularly strong motive for someone to kill Gasthorpe."

"The problem is, until we know what's in the papers, everyone could possibly have had a motive," said Fina, pushing out her lower lip so her sigh ruffled the fringe on her forehead.

Wendell replied, "I agree, but let's not get overwhelmed by that at this stage. Let's keep going through the suspects, even if it seems rather vague at this point. Who did you talk to at dinner, Fina? Let's keep going in that order."

"I first spoke to Grace Yingxia. She didn't seem particularly nervous. But..." Fina stared at the stuffed boar's head above the fireplace.

"Feens? Did she do something odd?" enquired Ruby.

Wendell raised an eyebrow at the nickname. "'*Feens?*'"

Ruby gave out a little hiccough of a laugh. "Well, I call you 'Wendy', don't I?" Wendell looked like an embarrassed child, eyes facing downward.

Pixley's chin wobbled as a colossal laugh erupted from his belly.

"Go on, *Feens*," Pixley said to Fina.

Fina could feel her face was doing some sort of gymnastics on its own. Should she reveal the story about the thefts? She decided she could start it, but then let Ruby make the decision as to whether she could trust Pixley with the dean's appeal to their sleuthing skills.

"Grace didn't have any theories about the murder, and she didn't seem troubled by it. But she did say someone had been stealing her poems."

"You mean plagiarism?" suggested Wendell.

"No, literally stealing her poems – taking them from her room. As well as some other … items." She looked over at Ruby.

Ruby took the hint. She put a hand on Pixley's shoulder. "Pixley, I'm about to ask you to do something which is antithetical to your career. And to your nature. I want you to sit on a story."

"What? What story?" asked Pixley, beginning to jiggle his leg so much the table began to quiver.

"Indeed. I can promise you an exclusive if we ever solve this mystery, along with the murder. Promise to keep it a secret?"

Pixley held his hand over his heart. Fina looked behind his back to make sure he wasn't crossing his fingers.

"Promise," he said.

Ruby relayed the story of the college pilferer. Wendell and Pixley, despite their life experiences, looked wholly engrossed and somewhat scandalised.

When Ruby had finished, she said, "So now we add Grace to the list of victims."

Wendell began to scribble notes – ostensibly about the thefts – in his notebook. Leaning in to see, Ruby said to him, "Why are you adding in notes about this? It's unrelated to the murder."

Wendell tapped his teeth with his pencil. "I'm not so sure. Fina, the way you talked about it made it seem like you were suspicious in some way of Grace's story – is that correct?"

"I suppose so. It struck me as odd that she was telling me this story. She'd only just met me yet she's telling me someone is stealing her poems – and she hasn't even notified the dean."

Pixley nodded. "I agree with Feens." Fina winced at his use of her nickname, but then told herself to lighten up.

"So I'll put a little star next to Grace's name with a note about the college thief," said Wendell. Ruby nodded her approval.

"I also spoke to Enid. Now, Enid didn't see anything, and I

cannot say she had any kind of motive I can fathom – except some personal vendetta," said Fina, pausing. "However, she did talk about Vera. She said Vera had been more spiteful lately, which is hard to believe because she's been nothing but venomous since I've met her."

"Tell us how you really feel about her, Fina," said Pixley, smiling.

She gave him a sheepish smile. "Well, in any case, Enid is practically stuck to Vera like a limpet, so she does have a sense of her moods. And apparently she's been much more moody lately."

"You don't think it's..." Wendell trailed off.

Ruby gave her brother a little punch in the arm. "No, silly, leave your ideas about women out of it. I'm sure Enid has the most accurate view of Vera's moods and behaviour. So what's causing it?"

Fina shook her head. "Maybe her infatuation with Esmond is cooling off? Maybe family or school troubles? It could be anything. She's so wrapped up in herself that anything which goes wrong takes on epic proportions. And yet I don't believe she'd have the planning skills to carry through a murder like this one."

"I'm not sure. I think there's a very clever brain underneath that narcissistic personality," said Ruby.

"Perhaps," replied Fina. "And I can imagine relatively small slights could become something big enough in her mind to justify murder."

Pixley yawned conspicuously. "I had an early start this morning to work on a story. If you all don't mind, I need to freshen up before we make our way to the train station," he said, stowing his cigarette case in his jacket pocket. "I'm fortunate my room is right upstairs." He rose from his seat and Ruby moved aside so he could squeeze through.

Ruby let out a great stream of air as he trundled off toward the stairs. Her shoulders slumped a little.

"I enjoy Pixley enormously," she said by way of explanation to Wendell, "But I don't feel like I can be completely in the open with him. I'm glad we have a few minutes to chat alone."

26

Wendell pursed his lips. "Pixley is a good chap. Completely trustworthy, but I do agree his journalistic nose could cause us some trouble."

"You don't think he's the one sent down to spy on us, do you, Ruby?" asked Fina.

Wendell looked horrified. "Surely it has to be someone else. I've known Pixley a long time."

"But you know as well as I do the government – or other organised interests – can threaten perfectly decent people in order to compel them to do things they find abhorrent."

Wendell shook his head. "Not Pixley. You've read his stories – he's completely on our side."

"Nevertheless..." said Ruby. "But let's leave that aside for a moment and talk about Pixley's possible involvement in the murder."

Fina said, "The only thought I have is they're both journalists. Perhaps Gasthorpe stole one of Pixley's stories? It certainly seems like something he would have done."

"Yes, but it's scarcely grounds for murder," said Wendell.

"Political motives? After all, you said he's on the same side as us," replied Fina.

"No," said Wendell firmly. "I cannot imagine that. Pixley is a courageous chap in the sense of the written word and taking risks to his life, but not courageous in the sense of putting himself voluntarily in any kind of direct danger."

Ruby tapped her coaster on the table. "I agree Pixley seems an unlikely suspect. Let's move on to James – I spoke to him at dinner."

Wendell's pencil hovered over the notebook, poised for action.

"Well, we know James is a history student like myself," said Fina.

"And he has quite a crush on Gayatri at the moment," said Ruby.

"And possibly Vera as well," said Fina.

"Agreed, though he seems genuinely confused about that."

Fina leaned back in her chair with a smile on her face. "He seems like a confused sort of chap all round. When we went to Professor Bathurst's lecture – you remember, Ruby, the time he was so rude to you – that was the day I saw James eating paper."

Wendell and Ruby gazed at her as if she were an exotic animal. "You mean ... what do you mean?" asked Wendell.

Fina explained James' peculiar diet that day in lecture. "And the strange thing was, all the bits he tore off had to be exactly circular, or as near as he could get considering the paper was square."

"Intriguing," said Wendell. "Jimmy Gates. A friend of mine in the navy. Used to eat paper, too – and it wasn't for lack of food. It's called xylophagia."

"I'm impressed," said Fina. "You mean it's a clinical condition?"

Wendell nodded. "Psychologists argue it's a type of nervous tic, or a way to cope with strain. But medical doctors think it's a sign of some sort of nutrient deficiency."

Ruby squeezed Wendell's arm and gave a nod toward him as she looked at Fina. "That's my brother, Feens. A walking encyclopaedia."

"You're absolutely spiffing, Wendell. Between your knowledge, Ruby's analytical mind and my photographic memory, we make quite the team!"

Wendell beamed. He picked up his pencil again. "What else do we know about James's background? Does he have money like Vera?"

"I know he is from New Zealand. His parents split up because of intense social discrimination pressures in that country. From what I've gathered, he more or less escaped to England with a scholarship to Oxford. He seems like a naïve, sweet puppy on the surface, but when I mentioned New Zealand politics he revealed a new side to his personality," said Fina.

"Such as?" asked Wendell.

"Hard and calculating. Very passionately committed. No wonder, given what his family has been through."

Ruby jumped a little in her seat. "What if he was testing you – by spouting these beliefs with the hope you'd agree. What if he is the one spying on us?"

"It did occur to me," said Fina, "Especially because he is new to the college and was so vehemently committed to his politics. I decided to hold my cards close to my chest and just politely and blandly ignored his comments. Even though I had a book in my arms which suggested otherwise. He eventually gave up."

"So he had the same opportunity as everyone else," said Wendell. "The only motive we have for him is that Gasthorpe was a dedicated advocate of colonialism, and James is not." He rubbed his chin. "It seems unlikely he would be spying on you two, given his politics."

"Agreed," said Ruby. "And I can really only see him killing Gasthorpe in a fit of rage. I think the rage would make it impossible for him to plan in advance."

"But you said he was hard and calculating," said Wendell. "Isn't that the perfect type to plan a murder?"

Ruby sighed. "If the motive were political, I think James would act out of immediate anger. Of course, if he has some other motive, I do think he could plan it."

"I'll put a little star next to his name," said Wendell with a grin.

"So who do we have left on our list?" asked Fina.

Wendell looked down at the page. "Gayatri, Dean Ossington, Professor Marlston and, of course, you two."

The pub was beginning to empty out. The grandfather clock in the corner chimed half past ten.

"Wendy, you know the two of us didn't do it," Ruby said.

He grinned. "You know I know that to be true, but I do think it's worth talking about."

Fina's gut began to tie up in knots. "Well, the police certainly seem to think I'm the number one suspect."

Wendell looked at her with an intensely focused gaze. "Then how can we make them think otherwise?"

"I suppose the key is to find those papers. Then we'll know more about who else might be implicated," said Ruby. "Right now all the motives are rather weak, except for Fina's."

"Then let's double up on the search for the papers and the college thief tomorrow," said Fina.

"I agree, but let's review Gayatri, Marlston and the dean before we make our way to the station," said Ruby.

"Well, I'd say Gayatri is completely in the clear, except for the fact she was behaving oddly in the chemistry laboratory today," said Fina. "But I suppose she could be doing a bit of sleuthing on her own."

Ruby nodded. "And Victoria? She seems unlikely as well. Remember, she and Grace were trying to talk the dean out of bringing Gasthorpe to the college – wasn't that how their conversation went – that night at dinner?"

"Exactly. Victoria is like the others – she doesn't have an apparent motive. She's a strong women's equality advocate, but I think her politics lean more toward the anti-colonial rather than pro-colonial side," said Fina. "And she's so fussy I cannot imagine her taking a risk like one would have to in carrying out the murder. Making it up as you go along is anathema to her. I remember how upset she became last term when she didn't finish her lecture in time. Are you listening, Ruby?"

Fina jogged her friend's elbow, and Ruby came out of her trance with a jolt. Frowning, she replied, "That's a thought ... yes, it gives me an idea. And another thing. We also overheard that odd conversation today, remember?" Ruby turned to Wendell to explain. "It seemed to hint at some sort of romantic relationship between the two of them, Grace and Victoria – right, Feens?"

Wendell's eyes grew larger, but he continued to scribble in his notebook.

Fina nodded. "And if Gasthorpe knew about it, it could be a motive. But it seems unlikely."

"That leaves the dean," said Fina. "Now, she was the one who invited Gasthorpe, so that automatically gives her a head start on the planning."

"Yes. And we know Quenby is in need of money."

Fina's breath quickened. "And Gasthorpe was supposed to possibly give her funds that evening if the party was a success."

Ruby tapped the coaster again. "Yes. And the missing will.

The dean is the one person – besides yourself, dear one – who has a strong motive for the crime related to money."

Fina sighed. Her excitement vanished. "The only problem is killing him would surely stop the flow of funds into the college purse."

27

The neon sign of the White Rabbit flashed at their merry party, not because it was supposed to do so, but because something was clearly wrong with the wiring. Ruby led the way, pushing open the small door into a darkened corridor. She waved her friends in behind her and they all moved in single file, away from the all-too-quiet alleyway.

As her eyes adjusted to the gloom, Fina could hear the muffled sounds of drums, saxophone and piano coming from somewhere below. Everyone walked on their tiptoes, as if they might be discovered, or even disturb the band. They made their way down a winding staircase to a velvet green curtain at the base. Wendell emerged from the back of the line and pushed through to the front. He whispered something into the ear of a person with the bulk of a rugby player. Nodding, he pulled back the curtain to let them all pass through.

Fina gave out a little gasp at the size of the room. While it wasn't gigantic, it was certainly much larger than anyone could imagine from outside in the alleyway. A small band of musicians, clad in white suits and black bowties, played a gentle ballad on stage. She could tell by the sheen of sweat on the foreheads of some of the guests this was merely an interlude from the energetic jazz they'd been playing for most of the night. Couples swayed in each other's arms. Most looked to be holding one another up rather than embracing.

Crash.

Fina, along with everyone else in the club, turned to see James on the floor next to an overturned table.

"Sorry, everyone. Should have worn my eyeglasses," he said, holding up his hand in mock surrender.

Wendell dashed over and hoisted him up. As he did so, he nodded to the man who had peeked in through the green velvet curtain to make sure no one needed to be removed.

Ruby let out a noticeable sigh. So much for their subtle entrance, thought Fina. But as she looked around the room, no one seemed to care. Fina could see why they had chosen this club. Most of the patrons were not white-British. The gleam in Vera's eye revealed she thought this was rather exciting. Fina cursed Vera for her prejudice and then she cursed herself for judging her, or more precisely, for thinking she was any different from or superior to Vera.

A waiter led the party to some tables in the back, clearly a precautionary measure in case they were to make any more disruptive noise. As they sat down and began to readjust their clothes, Fina surveyed each member of their gathering a little more closely. The goal of the outing was to see Vera in action – whatever that meant – but it seemed worthwhile to also scrutinise the others.

Wendell sat across from her, looking as cool and nonchalant as ever in his sharp but casual suit. The band struck up a raucous version of *Some of These Days* and a slow smile of pleasure eased across his countenance. Vera, next to Wendell, was tapping her foot and wriggling in her seat. She wore a red velvet gown and her eye makeup was by far the most dramatic of their crowd. Whenever Fina had tried that type of eye makeup in the past, she generally looked like a raccoon who had had a late night. Vera turned to Wendell and pointed to the dance floor. Soon they were off, lost in the crowd. They were both fantastic dancers.

Pixley tapped Fina on the shoulder.

"Care to dance?" he asked, twirling his spectacles.

"I'd love to, but after I've had a drink."

"Sounds about right to me," he said with a wink. "What can I get you?" He rose from his seat.

"Tom Collins, please," she said, rummaging around in her clutch for some cash. Pixley shook his head and smiled. "You can get the next round," he said as he walked off toward the long bar with two overworked-looking bartenders behind it.

Fina returned to her task. She peered at James. He wore the same suit he had worn to dinner. Perhaps it was one of the few suits he owned. He was staring with that lost-in-the-stars look again at Gayatri. Gayatri, on the other hand, was gazing out at the dancers and grinning in between sips of her gin and tonic. Instead of her usual brown motif, she wore a burgundy chiffon gown which suited her well. Fina thought that must have been the work of her fashionable sister, Sajida. Pixley returned with her Tom Collins. The mellow sweetness slid down her throat. She began to feel brave enough to chance the dancefloor.

Ruby and Pixley were dancing now. Ruby wore a gold lamé gown that was stunning. She looked rather like a swan next to Pixley, who was having the time of his life simply jumping up and down without a care about whether his jumping was timed to the music.

Fina leaned over to Enid, who was sipping lemonade. Fina couldn't tell if she were puckering her lips from the lemons or from her disapproval of this club. In her simple skirt and jumper, the girl looked as if she were attending a lecture. She did pull back her hair, however, in a way that made her glamour factor rise a bit. In between the puckered lips and gulps of her drink, Fina thought she could detect the slightest smile of enjoyment peeking out from behind the mask.

Wendell had returned, triumphant. Vera retook her seat with a reddish cocktail. She leaned back in her seat after taking a long drag on her cigarette. But no sooner had the band struck up *Nobody's Sweetheart Now* than Wendell was on his feet again. Surprisingly – although not so surprisingly, given what Fina had seen of Wendell's sensitive nature – he asked Enid to dance. Even more amazingly, Enid accepted his offer. Soon they were out on the floor. It took a good two minutes for Enid to warm up, but before long her arms were waving every which way and she had a glowing smile on her face. Fina couldn't help but wave at her with pleasure.

James leaned over and whispered something into Gayatri's ear. She smiled and shrugged. Soon the two of them were on the dance floor. While Gayatri danced next to James, Fina wouldn't say she exactly danced *with* him. She looked at her feet, looked at the other dancers or the band – anywhere but James. Of course, he had eyes only for her.

Before Fina knew what was happening, she found herself out on the floor, dancing with Pixley. Pixley was an excellent dance partner because she was entirely – well, almost entirely – unself-conscious when she danced with him. If only she could dance more often; it was one of the few times her brain turned off from its constant cycle of worrying thoughts. As she spun around, she could see the table was empty. Vera had been there a minute ago, contemplating her own smoke rings. She must have gone to the bathroom to freshen up.

As the next song turned out to be a slow ballad interval, Fina skipped back to the table with her fellow dancers. Everyone was seated now, enjoying an excited chat or hurried gulps of their cocktails. Fina quickly drained two glasses of water.

That was odd. She had seen Gayatri disappear into the bathroom corridor almost twenty minutes ago – at least that was how long ago it seemed to be. She was the only one missing from their table. Perhaps something was wrong. Fina rose and made her way to the blue velvet curtain in the back which hid the bathrooms.

She pulled it back and screamed.

Gayatri lay on the floor.

Wendell and Ruby were the first ones by her side. Wendell bent down and said quietly, "Gayatri? Can you hear me?"

He gently lifted her head and took her pulse. By now, a small crowd had formed around them. James moved forward with a glass of water. Wendell waved it away impatiently.

"Please, everyone, move back. She needs to breathe."

Fina let out a sigh of relief that sounded more like a groan. Gayatri was still alive.

Wendell said again, "Gayatri."

Her wide brown eyes flickered and opened. "What happened? I—"

"Shhh," said Wendell.

"Don't shhh me, Wendell," said Gayatri.

Wendell gave her a wry smile. "I'm glad to see you haven't lost your sense of dignity, Gayatri. Let me help you sit up." He held her back and lifted her up so she could sit. "Where's that glass of water?"

James moved forward with the glass. "I say, what happened, Gayatri?"

Wendell frowned at him, but said nothing.

Gayatri rubbed her forehead with the effort of remembrance. "I– I– I just went to the bathroom. As I opened the door to the ladies' room and entered, everything went black."

She made an attempt to rise to her feet, then another. "Are you sure you don't want to stay sitting?" asked Wendell.

"No, no," said Gayatri with a forced smile. "I'll be fine. Everyone can go back to dancing," she said as Wendell helped her to her feet – successfully, this time.

As everyone made their way back to the table, Ruby wiggled her finger at Fina for her to follow. She gestured upwards, so Fina picked up her coat and clutch. As they made their way up the dark stairs, Fina said, "We aren't going to leave them there, are we?"

"No. I told Wendell to ask them all to leave after the next two songs. We'll all meet at the entrance. I wanted a minute to talk to you."

"Brrr..." said Fina, shivering as they stepped into the blessedly fresh air. Well, as fresh as it ever was in London. "Now," she said, turning to Ruby. "What just happened in there? Who attacked Gayatri?"

Ruby pulled the lapels of her coat up so her voice became a muffled whisper.

"We cannot tell anyone. And we certainly cannot confront her."

"Ruby Dove, if you do not tell me right now, I shall burst. And that is not a pretty sight."

Ruby grinned. "Keep your shirt on, Feens," she said, with another infuriating dramatic pause.

"It was Vera."

28

After a rather bleary-eyed breakfast the next morning, Fina and Ruby made their way to Vera's room.

Fina half carried, half dragged, the bags full of Vera's gowns. They were finally complete. If she could get through the next few minutes in Vera's presence, she wouldn't have to openly interact with her any further. She did feel like she had the upper hand, though, since the dress unveiling provided a convenient excuse to confront Vera about her violent behaviour last night.

Instead of her usual gliding motion, Ruby's step seemed a little more leaden this morning. Hardly surprising given how late they had stayed up the night before. Fina held her woozy head.

As they approached Vera's door along a long corridor, Fina noticed how preternaturally quiet it was. There were a number of rooms along the corridor and yet it was completely silent.

Ruby tapped on Vera's door. Fina could feel cold air streaming out, over her ankles.

No answer.

Ruby knocked.

Silence.

Then she banged at it again.

Fina's heart began to race, even though she said in a calm voice that was surely not her own, "Must be sleeping."

"But do you feel cold air at your feet? The window must be wide open inside."

"Maybe she likes to sleep with oodles of fresh air?" said Fina, not believing her own statement for a moment.

"Let's find a scout," said Ruby. "I'm worried."

Beatrice was wandering the halls, picking up errant pieces of linen from the bathrooms. Fina thought her trembling curls looked a little less, well, curly today. Must be her own overactive imagination. In times of strain, Fina fixated on the most insignificant details around her – such as someone's hair. It had come in handy in their past cases, she had to admit.

Ruby strode up to Beatrice. "Miss Truelove, we're concerned about Vera Sapperton's well-being. We've knocked on her door – loudly – several times. There's no answer."

"Well, that one has a wicked night life, if you ask me," said Beatrice. "Comes in all hours and sleeps in late. I know, because she often comes in past curfew and I have to get up and let her in," she said, shaking her head. "When she came in last night, it was gone one o'clock. Still sound asleep, like as not."

Ruby stood still. Waiting.

Beatrice looked up at her. "Oh, very well," she said, fishing out an enormous key ring. It looked like enough keys for a castle, thought Fina.

Beatrice led them down the hall.

Tap, tap.

"Miss Sapperton. It's Beatrice. Beatrice Truelove. Are you in there?" She banged on the door. Heads began to pop out of doors down the corridor.

Beatrice began to flip through her keys, one by one. Selkies and kelpies, thought Fina. We'll be here all day.

Finally, she held up the key in triumph and plunged it into the lock.

Cold air hit them in the face. All the windows were wide open.

Fina looked around the familiar mess of Vera's room. Clothes were strewn everywhere, covering books, papers and boxes. There was a thin layer of ash in the fireplace, indicating it hadn't been used that often. This made sense since Vera probably wasn't in her room very frequently.

The beds in college were set off in a little recess, so you could only see someone lying in bed if you came all the way into the room. As they approached the middle of the room, or nearly stumbled in the case of Fina, who had a tangle with some clothes on the floor, they saw Vera.

She lay in bed, one arm over her chest and the other arm outstretched over the side of the bed, as if she were dancing the tango in her sleep. But this was not sleep.

It was death.

~

Fina rubbed her eyes. She'd had plenty of strong tea, so she knew she was awake. This couldn't be happening again.

She went over to Ruby and gave her a side embrace, as much for herself as for her friend. Beatrice sat on her haunches in front of the bed. She felt Vera's outstretched hand for a pulse. Then she shook her head and removed her cap.

Vera's lifeless eyes stared at a small oil painting on the opposite wall. It was of a landscape – it looked like the English countryside. Perhaps it was where she grew up. A little pang of regret hit Fina as she recalled all the awful things she had thought about Vera.

She was shaken from her reflection by Ruby's action. Her

friend moved toward the bed, bending over Vera's face. Then she looked on the nightstand. There was a little silver snuffbox next to a hairbrush, water glass, notebook and small clock. After poking her nose into the teacup, Ruby pulled out her favourite blue handkerchief her grandmother in St Kitts had given her. She used it to pick up the silver snuff box.

"You'd better leave that be, Miss Dove," said Beatrice, not unkindly.

"Don't worry, Miss Truelove," said Ruby, first smelling the contents. "I've had experience with this – and I won't disturb any fingerprints."

Then she inserted her pinky finger into the snuffbox and transferred a tiny dab of its contents to her mouth.

"Ruby! What on earth are you doing? It could be poison," said Fina.

She shook her head. "Don't worry, I had a tiny smidge to confirm what I thought."

"What is it?"

"Cocaine."

Beatrice, who had still been sitting on her haunches, fell over onto the floor.

"Cocaine?" she sputtered. "You're having me on!"

Fina and Ruby bent over to help Beatrice to her feet.

"It must not be that out of the ordinary for a scout to come across drug usage in college."

"Well, yes, I've heard of these things. But not in a *women's* college," breathed Beatrice.

"I'm afraid addiction does not respect gender roles, Miss Truelove," said Ruby.

Fina leaned over and whispered to Ruby. "Is that why she hit Gayatri on the head last night? Do you think Vera was trying to buy more cocaine?"

Ruby whispered back, "I think so, but it was more than that.

Remember the bag Vera carried last night? Very unfashionable for someone like her. I think she had some of the stolen jewellery in there and was trying to trade that for drugs. It may even have been Gayatri's necklace. I don't think she would have assaulted Gayatri just to keep her from seeing her buy drugs. It was to keep Gayatri from realising she was the college thief."

As Beatrice stood there in shock, Ruby and Fina made the most of her distraction. They began to search the room – just with their eyes. Ruby grabbed Fina's arm and pointed silently.

There, in the corner, sat a heap of women's underclothes. Fina whispered, "She was a terrible pack rat. Perhaps it's her own clothing?"

"There's only one way to find out for certain whether she was the college thief," replied Ruby as she marched over to the pile. She picked up the nearest white brassiere and held it across her chest. "What do you think? We were probably about the same size, though I'm taller."

The brassiere was clearly not made for the likes of Ruby or Vera.

Next, Ruby selected a pair of knickers, barely touching them. Beatrice still stood transfixed, staring at Vera's body.

Ruby gave the knickers to Fina. "You were closer in size to her knickers." Fina held them up to her. They were enormous. Ruby began to giggle.

Beatrice whirled round to see Fina holding up the pants to her waist. The look of horror on her face prompted a snort of laughter from Fina. Must be the shock, she thought to herself, trying not to feel ashamed.

"Wait until I tell the police about your behaviour, young ladies!" said Beatrice as she marched out of the room.

They followed her out like children who had been scolded by the headmistress.

Beatrice turned the key in the lock.

29

"Good grief," murmured Ruby. "This tea is dreadful. Tastes like dishwater."

Fina looked down into the brown liquid which passed as tea in the local police station. She sighed and decided she'd better drink it. She might not get anything else to drink for a while.

Constable Clumber wandered toward them, playing with a lighter by swinging it open, igniting it, and then flipping it shut.

"The chief inspector will see you now. Please follow me," he said with a little wave. Fina thought he looked utterly ridiculous in the constable uniform. Not for the first time, it struck her that making police appear ludicrous would scarcely achieve the stated police goal of respect for authority. Authority, my foot.

She followed Ruby dutifully down the hallway, filled with what she surmised were typical smells of a police station. Stale coffee and tea, sweat, plenty of sweat, dust and the smell of gently rotting paper. She tried to focus on Ruby's self-assuredness so she wasn't overwhelmed by the odour. It brought back unpleasant memories of her long afternoon in the station.

They arrived at a windowless room with four rickety chairs and an even more perilous-looking table. In the corner sat a small table with cups holding the remnants of previous guests' tea and coffee. A single lightbulb, suspended from a wire in the ceiling, buzzed as if it were ready to burn out.

Hogston now had an actual beard. His eyes were sunken and his skin had a sickly sheen from poor nutrition and even poorer sleep. Much of this was obscured by his homburg, which was beginning to look the worse for wear. Snorscomb, on the other hand, stroked his pencil moustache and looked like a man anticipating a delicious meal.

Snorscomb motioned to the pair to take a seat, whistling a children's song Fina couldn't place. Clumber gave a little bow and floated out of the room, his cape making little flapping noises as he did so.

Poised as ever, Ruby sat with her handbag on her lap. Fina slung her small satchel across the back of her chair. Not knowing what to do with her hands, she followed Ruby's lead and folded them in her lap.

"Thank you for coming, Miss Aubrey-Havelock and Miss Dove," said Hogston, leaning back in his chair.

As if we had a choice in the matter, thought Fina bitterly. She was doing her best not to let the questioning bring back those terrible memories of police interviews about her father's murder. Earlier, she had discussed this with Ruby, and Ruby had agreed it was better if she took the lead in the questioning for this reason, as well as the fact that Fina was clearly more of a suspect than Ruby.

Ruby relayed the details of what had happened that morning, precisely and succinctly. Snorscomb looked grateful as he scribbled.

"Thank you, Miss Dove, that's very helpful. I assume you agree with this account, Miss Aubrey-Havelock?"

Fina nodded.

"Right. Let's move on to the question of the cocaine. May I

ask you, Miss Dove, how you knew the substance in the snuff box was cocaine?"

"I'm a chemistry student, Chief Inspector. And cocaine is not that unusual. Besides, it is quite common for wealthy English people to constantly ask for cocaine in the Caribbean. That's why I'm familiar with it."

"I see," he said, looking a little sheepish.

Hogston removed a yellowing handkerchief from his breast pocket and wiped his brow. "Now, Miss Aubrey-Havelock and Miss Dove, we come to the curious incident of the, er, ladies' undergarments. Miss Truelove told us you were picking through a pile of these underclothes on the floor and holding them up to yourselves. To make matters worse, you apparently found these events to be worthy of a laugh. Can you explain yourselves?"

"I'll start with the laughter. As you can understand, Fina and I have been under a stupendous strain over the past few days. I understand one reaction to shock can be laughter. I believe that's what happened. Everything seemed suddenly absurd," she said. Fina nodded agreement.

"But it is true you were not on friendly terms with the deceased?"

Fina jumped in, unable to help herself. "Miss Sapperton was a narcissist of the highest order, Chief Inspector. She was difficult to take at the best of times."

"Precisely," said Ruby. "And you mustn't forget she had been even more moody lately, most likely due to her cocaine habit. We spent twice as long as we normally would preparing her gowns because she rejected every change we made multiple times, even when she had requested the change herself earlier."

"Hmmm," was all the chief inspector said, but there was a glint in his eye which suggested he understood. "But why in heaven's name were you looking at her– her—" He cleared his throat. "Her underclothes?"

"You see, Chief Inspector, the college has a thief. A rather innocuous thief. At least innocuous in comparison with a murderer," said Ruby. "Not that it's murder – it's an overdose. But the first death was clearly murder."

"You'd better start from the beginning, Miss Dove," said Hogston.

Ruby did as he requested. At the end of her monologue, Hogston asked, "Why didn't you two tell us this earlier? This is a murder investigation!" He banged his fist on the table.

Fina and Ruby both jumped in their seats. Even Snorscomb looked disconcerted.

Ruby licked her lips and sat up a little straighter. "I know we both understand the gravity of the situation, but yelling is most undignified."

Hogston rose out of his seat. Snorscomb put a hand on his arm, but he flung it off as if his subordinate were trying to entrap him. After a few paces around the room, the chief inspector returned to his seat, visibly calmer.

"I'm sorry for my outburst, Miss Dove, but I am even more sorry you withheld evidence from the police. You understand the seriousness of this matter?"

Tap, tap.

Constable Clumber's head peeked around the door.

"Yes, what is it, Clumber? We're in the middle of an interview."

"Sorry, sir, but there's a Lieutenant Dove to see you. He says it's urgent."

In the blessedly fresh air of the early evening, Fina, Ruby, and Wendell stood on the steps outside the police station. Hazy twilight made the red and orange leaves on the trees glow. Fina pulled up her jacket collar as protection against the chill in the air.

"What kind of banana oil did you feed them to get us out of that filthy police station?" asked Ruby.

Wendell pulled out his silver cigarette case. He took a long drag on his Woodbine before he answered. "I told them they couldn't hold you for questioning as they had absolutely no evidence against you, especially because they had yet to confirm this was a murder. I reminded Hogston of the letter from Captain Marshall I gave to him. I said I could ask the captain to call the station and tell them to release you two – if he wanted to go down that route. Hogston immediately began to simper. It was rather pathetic, but it was effective."

Fina was impressed. Wendell must be doing something special to receive that kind of recommendation from the captain.

As if he could intuit Fina's thoughts, Wendell offered, "I asked Captain Marshall to write me a letter of introduction of sorts. He's an obliging chap. I need it because my navy papers are not enough to convince certain English people I am competent – or that I am who I say I am."

Ruby put an understanding hand on Wendell's arm.

With a slow smile, he continued, "Hogston also told me the dean sought you two out as super sleuths. To solve *the case of the college pilferer*," he said in a dramatic voice. "He wanted to know if I knew why the dean had asked you two to sleuth."

Fina held her breath. "What did you tell him?"

"I said you two had happened to be around when I did some light intelligence work – nothing top secret – and that you had proved helpful in the past. I said the dean must have found out about that and requested your help because she wanted to avoid public scandal for the college."

"We must tell the dean all this before the police question her again," said Ruby. "We need to make sure we have our stories straight."

Wendell nodded as he stepped on his cigarette. "Right. You two should go along to tell her while I stay here. I want to ask the chief inspector a few more questions."

Ruby gave him a hug and looked up at him. "Do be careful, Wendy. That lieutenant's cap won't save you from police harassment. Or worse."

"I know – and I do appreciate the concern. You two ought to be careful, too. It won't be long before the news of this rather salacious murder makes its way around the college – you might be in danger."

The pair turned to go. Wendell said, "Blast it. I almost forgot to tell you the most important titbit I picked up from Hogston."

"Yes?" said Ruby.

"It wasn't an overdose. The cocaine was laced with a poison. Most likely nicotine."

30

Fina clutched her stomach. Wendell's revelation had been sickening news – but there was another reason for the nausea which was suddenly flowing over her. "Ruby, I cannot take this in. And I'm famished. Aren't you?" she asked in a rather pathetic-sounding voice as the pair made their way back to college.

Ruby looked at her watch. "Hmmm ... dinner in college is almost over. I have a topping idea! Follow me."

And like a small dog following a chain of linked sausages, Fina hurried on through the night.

Soon they arrived at a small shop, aglow with a fire and candles. "It looks like a shop – and it is a confectionery – but they also serve tea and the most succulent cakes you'll find in Oxford," said Ruby before opening the door, which gave a little merry tinkle as they entered.

Fina promptly forgot everything. The murder, the knickers, her papers, everything.

"How did you find this magical place and why haven't you told me about it, Miss Ruby Dove?" said Fina in a mock-scolding voice.

"It opened last month. I wanted to surprise you with it for a special occasion. This wasn't what I had in mind exactly, but it is a rather out-of-the-ordinary event."

"Murder is becoming a little more ordinary than I'd like to admit!"

They approached the glass case displaying the cakes. Ruby explained you went to the case to decide what you wanted and they would take the order from your table. As per usual, Fina was drawn to the chocolate items. Ruby couldn't decide between fruit and chocolate options.

Fina settled on something called "Decadent Death" and Ruby opted for the "Splendid Strawberry Tart". The cheerful woman who took their order told them that since it was near closing time, she'd give them each an extra-large slice.

Fina's mouth watered.

"I know you cannot focus until you've satiated that beast in your stomach, Feens. Frankly, neither can I," said Ruby, her eyes alight as the tray laden with enormous slices of cake and tart approached their table.

In between forkfuls of utter heaven, Fina mumbled, "So we have to tell the dean tonight."

Setting her fork down for a moment and dabbing the corners of her mouth, Ruby replied, "Yes. I don't believe Hogston will disturb her tonight – it's not important enough – but I'm sure he'll ask her tomorrow."

The strong, milky tea cleansed Fina's palate. Cleansed it so she could begin again! She shovelled another forkful in her mouth.

"And I do believe we have one other task we must complete tonight," said Ruby.

"Wass mat?" said Fina with her mouth full. She swallowed and repeated, "What's that?"

"I know it's probably crawling with police right now, but we must search the chemistry laboratory. We'll go later tonight, after we've spoken to the dean."

Fina replied with a smile, "I'll do anything you say now that I've had this cake!"

~

FINA TAPPED on the dean's door. "Do you think it's too late?" she whispered.

"Normally I would say yes, but these are extraordinary circumstances," said Ruby.

This time, Fina's tapping was more assertive.

Dean Ossington opened the door. Her eyes lit up at the sight of them, as if they were long-lost relatives.

"It's you! Please, please do come in. I was reading my book and having my usual cocoa," she said. Then she added, as if this behaviour was somewhat scandalous, "I thought it would calm my nerves."

"Indeed," said Ruby in her best reassuring voice. "Fina and I just stuffed ourselves with cakes – now we both feel much better."

"Come, sit by the fire," said the dean.

The cup of cocoa was still steaming next to a book titled *The University*. Hmm, thought Fina, whatever it was, it didn't sound like the book she'd turn to in a crisis. She preferred mysteries, as long as they were light in tone, in these circumstances.

"Now, what news do you have for me? I hope it is something uplifting because I must say the news of the last forty-eight hours has been anything but that," said the dean, taking a sip of cocoa. As she put down her cup in the saucer, her eyes grew wide. "I've completely forgotten my manners! May I offer you both a cup of tea?"

Ruby shook her head. "Thank you, no. We're all under a

great deal of strain. We're delighted you were able to see us tonight."

The dean leaned forward. "Yes, you two have been through quite an ordeal. I'm so glad to see the police did not keep you long at the station this time, Fina. The news about Vera's death has distressed me terribly. I know I shouldn't be worrying about the college right now, but this puts us in a very difficult position. Once this story gets out in the press – and it will tomorrow – we'll be the centre of attention, and not in a way I had hoped."

The dean still thought Vera's death had been accidental. Fina cleared her throat. "Dean Ossington, I'm afraid we have some more disturbing news. Vera didn't die of an overdose. Her cocaine was laced with nicotine. That means it was murder."

The dean's cocoa cup went flying across the room. Fortunately, it was empty, so the damage was minimal. As Fina and Ruby immediately sprang into action to clean up the minor mess, the dean's arms continued to flail about as if they belonged to some other being.

"This is disastrous. Who could have done such a thing? We're done for. Her people are enormously influential. Lord Fotherington. The university will close the college now, most certainly."

Getting back on her feet, Ruby went over to the dean and put an arm on her shoulder. "We're going to solve these murders, Dean Ossington. And I have a feeling that, once we do, all will be well with the college."

Sitting back down and smoothing her skirt, Ruby continued. "We didn't come only to give you this dreadful news. We also came to tell you we were forced to tell the police about our college thief."

Fina interjected. "You see, we found a pile of ladies' undergarments in the corner of Vera's room."

"And they were not her size," said Ruby.

The dean's eyes widened and she squeezed her lips together. "You mean Vera was the college thief?"

Ruby and Fina nodded in unison.

"My, my," said the dean. "How astonishing. Such a well-brought-up girl – from such a good family – I can hardly credit it. Do you think it was connected to a cocaine habit in some way?"

"It's possible, Dean Ossington, but I'm not sure how or why. Fina and I haven't had time to think about it, so we'll let you know as soon as anything comes to mind as a full explanation. I do think she returned the carriage clock because she knew she might be discovered."

The dean was calm now but Fina saw her right hand tremble. "What will the police think about us not telling them about the college thief? Do they think we were withholding evidence?"

"We told them you asked us to get involved with the investigation because we helped Ruby's brother with some investigations in the past. We made it clear we didn't mention it before because we thought it was irrelevant to the murder, and we didn't want to expose the college to scandal," said Fina.

The dean let out a sigh of relief. "Yes, I suppose that sounds like a believable reason why we didn't say anything," she said, twisting her pearl necklace. "I'm so glad the two of you came to notify me before the police questioned me again."

Ruby sat back in her chair. "Do you think someone wants this college to close? Is that a reasonable explanation for these murders?"

Now both of the dean's hands began to tremble. "It certainly seems plausible from my viewpoint, but I am rather prejudiced in that respect. You see, there's something I didn't tell you or the police."

Ruby and Fina leaned forward.

The dean lowered her voice. "I need scarcely remind you, my

dear girls, that I tell you this in utmost confidentiality. Not a word to a living soul."

They nodded.

"Before he died, the late Mr Gasthorpe told me that, in his will, he left the bulk of his estate to Quenby College. Unless the will resurfaces, however, the college will receive nothing."

31

"Crikey," said Fina as they left the dean's rooms.

"Indeed," said Ruby. "It does seem like a strong motive for murder if someone wanted to close the college. On the other hand, it seems like an awful lot of trouble and risk. You could more easily manufacture a series of other scandals."

"The only reason to suppress the will is if you were a relative of Gasthorpe's who would inherit," said Fina.

"Yes. But it would appear a little suspicious. Besides, as far as we know, no one has come forward yet to claim the inheritance."

"Early days, though. He died not that long ago."

"Good point, Feens. It feels like an eternity," said Ruby as they rounded the corner into their own quad.

"Look!" exclaimed Fina. "Isn't that Vera's room? I saw a flash of light from a torch."

"Could be the police," said Ruby.

"Why would they use a torch? Wouldn't they just turn on the lights?"

"You're right. Let's see if we can catch them!" said Ruby, slipping off her low heels. She began to run in her stockings toward the college door. Fina followed suit.

They crept up to Vera's door. Fina had a tiny pocket torch she used to lead them to the doorway. She shut it off and they were encased in complete darkness. Fina froze. Something was moving. She poked Ruby and pointed in the direction of the movement. Carefully, she swung the beam of the torch around. A furry face blinked up at them. Tibby! How did the grey ball of fluff find his way to this corridor? The scouts did their best to keep him out of the student rooms, but Tibby must have found a way to circumvent the rules, as was the case so often with cats.

Letting out a sigh of relief as silently as she could, Fina turned the torch back in the direction of Vera's room. She could see a small stream of light emanating from the crack created by an open door. She whispered to Ruby, "Why wouldn't the police have locked the door?"

"I'm sure they did," she whispered back. "It must be someone who has access to keys in college."

They both tiptoed, single file, to the far side of the door to listen.

Fina thought she recognised Professor Marlston's voice.

"Where can they be? They must be here under this mess."

"At least I found one notebook of my poems under a pile of clothes."

That must be Grace.

Then came more shuffling of feet, the slow slide of drawers, and the slight creaking of a door being opened.

"We've searched and searched. She must have hidden them elsewhere. It wouldn't surprise me if she had a stash hidden somewhere, since she clearly kept – or stole – everything."

Light footsteps approached the door.

Ruby and Fina dashed around the corner. They held their breath.

Fina could hear a key turning in the lock. Blast it. There went their chance to search Vera's room one more time.

Although presumably there was no longer any need, as the poet and the professor had already performed a thorough search.

They gently exhaled as Victoria and Grace tiptoed down the corridor in the opposite direction.

As they sat on the sofas in the main common room of the college, Fina felt herself nodding off. Even though the room was ablaze with light. This was the one room in college in which the lights were left on all day and night.

"Feens! Wake up. We still have work to do. I feel tired, too. It must be that the sugar is wearing off ... and it has been an exhausting day."

Fina rubbed her sore feet. "Must we really? I can barely move."

"Believe me, I know," said Ruby, returning the gesture. "But Grace and Victoria's search only confirms what we need to do. We must search the laboratory."

Fina nodded, her head flopping like a rag doll. "What do you think they were looking for?"

Ruby rubbed her nose. "You heard Grace. She was looking for her poems. Perhaps Victoria was also a victim of Vera's and was searching for her lost items."

"You forget, dear Ruby, that I know your tell – when you rub your nose. What is it you're keeping from me?" said Fina.

"I thought you were half asleep!" Ruby said with a mischievous grin. "But you're right. I do have a little theory, but it will have to keep. To marinate."

"Oh no, not marinating again. Does that mean you're getting close to solving the case?"

"Hardly, but I do feel like some pieces are starting to fall into place."

Fina knew better than to press Ruby for details. She'd have to wait until her friend was ready to reveal everything. Ruby could keep secrets. If she herself had even the slightest inkling of who had committed these murders, she would tell Ruby straight away. But then again, she didn't have the slightest inkling of who had committed these murders.

As they prepared for their nocturnal adventure, they opted for sensible plimsolls instead of heels.

Ruby fished out a key from a pocket of her frock as they padded along the corridor. She almost always sewed pockets into her own frocks – one of those important practical details which made Ruby a rising star in the fashion world.

The turn of the lock sounded deafening in the eerie silence of the corridor. Soon they were inside. The lab was lined with windows so the moon provided enough light to guide their way. Fina felt she would gag from the smell of various chemicals mixed together in a heady concoction. Thankfully, Ruby waved her towards the small closet they had seen earlier.

Fina turned her small torch on as Ruby shut the closet door behind them. She pulled out a second torch from her satchel and presented it to Ruby. The closet was much larger than it looked from the outside – it could comfortably have fit at least five people, if it weren't for the tables, boxes and chairs strewn about, making it into a storage closet. At the far end, Fina spied a small oil painting. Why did it seem familiar? That was it. The artist was the same one who'd created that oil painting in Vera's room. She moved closer to the painting. It was undoubtedly placed in a peculiar position. She removed it from the wall.

"Ruby!" she hissed. "Look!"

Ruby flashed her torch on the now-empty spot with a nail in the wall. A silver lock gleamed in the light.

Fina groaned. "It's a combination padlock."

She spun the numbered wheels fruitlessly. Click. Click.

Fina could hear Ruby tap her teeth.

"Let me try something," she said, moving toward the lock. Fina shone her torch as Ruby worked her magic.

"Blast it. I tried Bathurst's office number – 406. Perhaps..." She bent over the lock again. "No, not Vera's room number, either. Feens, have you got any ideas?"

Fina could only shake her head.

"There was something he told us," said Ruby. "If I could only ... Wait, it's coming to me ... aha! Let me try another. 1-2-8."

Selkies and kelpies. Success!

"What does 1-2-8 mean?"

"H-2-O. Hydrogen is number 1 on the periodic table, then 2, obviously, and then number 8 for oxygen on the periodic table."

"How on earth did you come up with that?"

"H-2-O equals water. Bathurst mentioned it when he was showing us around the lab. I thought it odd at the time, but I'm sure he enjoyed stumping us with a seemingly random reference."

They made their way inside the next closet. It was quite large as well, but it was filled with knick-knacks, trunks, and various other bits and bobs. As Fina shone her torch around the space, it lighted on a messy pile of pastel silk and lace. Women's undergarments! This must be where Vera hid everything she had stolen over the past few months.

In the opposite corner, Ruby's hand frantically waved her over. She had stopped at a wooden box and as Fina held the light steady, Ruby opened the lid. It was stuffed with papers. But that wasn't all. Fina saw a stack of two other boxes behind her. Ruby lifted the top off the next box, confirming that it, too, was packed with papers. The folders inside held newspaper clippings and scribblings about various people's personal lives.

"Who do they belong to?"

Ruby held up a letter. It was signed Harold Baden Gasthorpe.

They selected another letter at random. It was the same. All the notes in the folders were in the same handwriting – it must all belong to Gasthorpe.

Ruby gave Fina a glance of joy and exasperation. Selkies and kelpies! How could they look through all these papers tonight? They couldn't stay here, as the night porter might come through on his rounds – or perhaps even the police. And they certainly couldn't haul all these boxes back to their rooms without being noticed, let alone make multiple trips back and forth.

Fina opened the box nearest her and pulled out a few slips of paper at random. One read "Princess Goes Awry" and the other, "Businessman's Dubious Dealings". Fina sighed. But the third piece of paper made her nearly jump out of her skin. Though she could read only the top portion of the paper as the remainder was hidden in the box, the words "Dear Fina" caught her eye. She whipped the paper out of the box. Ruby, who had her back toward her, began to turn around. Fina hurriedly crumpled the paper and shoved it into her dress pocket. Time enough to read it later.

With an air of resignation, Ruby slid one of the tops of the boxes back into place.

She whispered, "We must notify the police about this. At least they can sort through the papers."

"You didn't see any papers related to the case in there?"

"No, but I'm quite certain they must be in there."

"Do we have to tell the police?"

Ruby nodded. "I know, I don't want to, either, but there may be a lot of confidential information in there we really shouldn't see. Besides, if they found out we were hiding this, you would be in even more danger than you are right now. We'll tell them in the morning."

As they made their way out of the closet, Fina saw a flash of light coming from the windows.

"Hurry!" she hissed. "It must be the night watchman on his rounds. Or the police!"

They scampered down the corridor in the opposite direction of the light. The doors were locked. Ruby waved her hand for Fina to follow her into a dark stairwell. She almost slipped on the well-worn staircase, but caught herself just in time by holding onto the railing.

She nearly fell down the stairs again as Ruby halted suddenly, just as they were reaching what looked to be a door.

"What is it?" asked Fina.

"Do you hear that noise?" Ruby stood still.

"It sounded like a scream," cried Ruby, running toward the door. Luckily, it swung open. They dashed onto the quad. The scream seemed to have come from there, but the closed-in walls created a deceptive echo effect.

At the archway nearest them, Fina could see a hooded figure gripping Professor Marlston painfully hard and shaking her, as Grace Yingxia stood next to her, trying to pry the attacker off her friend. As they got closer, they could hear foul language referring to women and women who love other women. "Bloody high-and-mighty man-hater..." the invective went on.

Fina spotted a broom standing at attention in the archway. Without thinking at all, she scooped it up and gave the attacker's legs a great whack. Then another. Ruby was by Victoria's side to catch her when she fell.

"Eeeeeee..." yelled the mysterious figure. He ran off, holding his hood in place tightly as he dashed out of the quad. Grace began to run after him. Ruby hissed, "Grace! Stay here!"

Reluctantly, she turned around with a look of fury on her face.

The three of them huddled around Professor Marlston. "Shall I call a doctor?" asked Ruby.

Victoria groaned and said, "No, I'll be fine. His bark was worse than his bite." She paused, looking at Fina. "Splendid batting, Miss Aubrey-Havelock." She turned to Ruby. "And thank you for stopping me from hitting my head on the ground."

"Who was it?" asked Fina.

"It was that– that—" Grace was gasping so heavily she could barely get the words out. "That *utter bastard* Esmond Bathurst!"

Ruby and Fina turned to stare at each other.

"Well, we must tell the police," said Fina. "They'll charge him with assault." Ruby looked at her quizzically. It was true, thought Fina, that the only solution which presented itself to her was to call the police. Despite everything she had been through with the blasted police, her first reaction was to call them in a crisis.

"I forbid you, Miss Aubrey-Havelock," said Victoria. "I do not want a scandal. It will cost me my job, not his."

"But he cannot get away with this!" cried Fina.

"There are other ways to ensure he does not do this again," said Grace quietly. Fina couldn't imagine what these other options might be but then again, this was Oxford. Backbiting politics at its highest and most original level.

"And you two must keep your mouths shut about our ... my..." Victoria said gruffly.

Grace's eyelids flickered. "What Victoria is trying to say is you must keep our relationship secret."

Ruby and Fina nodded in unison.

32

"Leave me be, Ruby!"

Fina pulled the counterpane further over her head. She squeezed herself into a little ball, like a threatened hedgehog.

"Please, go away. I feel awful. I never want to see anyone again," came the muffled entreaty from below the covers.

Fina felt a gentle pat on her shoulder. "Feens, what's wrong? I know the last few days have been dreadful, and dreadfully tiring. You know we have to go on to make sure you don't, you don't..." Ruby trailed off.

"I don't want to do anything. I'm through with everything," said Fina, like a petulant child.

Ruby didn't budge from her seat next to Fina on the bed.

Fina pulled back the covers and squinted. She could feel her hair sticking out every which way on her head. But she couldn't care one whit about it. And wouldn't care anymore. She reached over to the nightstand to retrieve the rumpled sheet of paper she had taken from the box in the closet last night and handed it to Ruby.

Ruby smoothed the paper and began to read aloud. Fina

intervened as she opened her mouth. "The letter is dated a month before Connor's execution."

Ruby's eyes widened as she began to read.

Dearest Fina,

Do not worry. I know you will anyway, but I hope this letter brings some sort of solace to you – as much as anything might. As our grandfather used to say, I've learned that honey is sweet, but one shouldn't lick it off a briar.

May those who love us, love us;
And for those who don't love us,
May God turn their hearts;
And if He doesn't turn their hearts,
May He turn their ankles,
So we will know them by their limping!

I have everything in hand. I've made peace with my fate. And until we meet again, may God hold you in the palm of his hand.

Your ever-loving brother,
Connor

Ruby's eyes glistened. She put an arm around Fina and said, "I'm so sorry, Feens. I can only imagine how difficult it is for you to read this. Did you find it in the box last night?"

Fina nodded. The tears flowed down her cheeks. Then she turned defiant. "I know most would read this as a definitive confession, but I believe he left me a message. Connor was always one for puzzles. He was forever trying his hand at crosswords."

Ruby's eyes scanned the letter again, rapidly. She nodded slowly. "It is possible, but it's going to take a great deal of work. And I'm afraid we have more urgent things to attend to, such as keeping you out of jail." She continued, "And I promise I will help you with it. You know I will."

As she got up from the bed, Fina said desperately, "You won't tell the police, will you? I know we must tell them about the boxes of papers, but we cannot tell them about this letter."

Ruby nodded in agreement.

After a hurried cold bath and some serious attention to her hair, Fina was on her way with Ruby to the café next to Wendell's inn for breakfast.

Crunch.

The café's toast was delicious. Fina gazed out of the window at Christ Church meadow, now denuded of flowers but with the evergreens dark like statues in the misty October sunshine. The landscape was so calm Fina could close her eyes and almost believe that none of the events of the past three days had occurred.

Almost.

When she opened her eyes, a flood of dread and anxiety streamed through her body. As her brain was wont to do, it skipped from worry to worry – not only the murder and her brother's letter, but more mundane worries such as missed lectures and late papers.

"Feens?" asked Ruby gently, as if she were waking her friend out of a deep sleep. "Would you like some more tea? They've brought us a lovely new pot."

Fina nodded and munched absently on her toast.

"Unfortunately," said Ruby, laying down her fork, "I have more news."

Wendell's mouth was filled with eggs but he swallowed

quickly, as if a full mouth would prevent him from listening carefully.

"Someone searched my room last night," Ruby said, crossing her arms.

"You mean while you were asleep?" gasped Fina. Toast crumbs fell all over the plate and her lap.

"No, no. I mean someone searched while we were searching the laboratory," she said. "I've already told Wendell the details of our escapade."

"Yes," said Wendell, "And I've notified the police about the boxes of documents and stolen goods you two found. Ruby and I thought it would be better if I relayed the news to the police. I reckoned it would create a sort of buffer between you and Hogston, who no doubt will be immediately outraged about the search. There should be enough time for him to cool down, and perhaps be somewhat grateful that you found – at least that's what we surmise – those missing documents."

He took a sip of tea and continued, "Was anything missing in your room, Ruby?"

Ruby smoothed her hair and dress. "Not that I could see. A couple of books: *Crime and Punishment*, *David Walker's Appeal*, and *Anna Karenina*. I was so infuriated that I cleaned everything and put it back in its place before I went to bed. Then, for good measure, I moved a wardrobe in front of my door – in case my night-time visitor decided to return."

No wonder Ruby looked haggard this morning; a word Fina would never normally associate with her friend.

"At least I am lucky enough to have the two of you to tell my troubles to. And it is a beautiful morning," she said, giving Wendell and Fina a little toast with her teacup.

It must be at least her sixth cup of tea, thought Fina.

Her own rather mushy brain felt like it could probably use another ten cups as well.

"So why did someone search your room?" enquired Wendell.

Ruby shrugged. "I suppose he or she thought I had Gasthorpe's papers myself, or wanted to frighten me. To be honest, if it were the latter, he didn't really succeed. I was more angry than frightened. Besides, if the culprit wanted to kill me, it wouldn't be that difficult."

Wendell pushed aside his clean plate and lit a cigarette. "What if the search is unconnected with the murder? What if it was the person sent down to spy on you two?"

Ruby grimaced as she pushed around the kedgeree in her bowl. Fina shuddered. There was nothing she disliked more than kedgeree. Reminded her of pig slop.

"Yes, I thought of that. But why now? Why take an extra risk of being caught when there's a murder investigation on?"

"Good point. But perhaps this person thinks it will have the effect of further incriminating you in some way," said Wendell.

"It's possible," said Ruby, doubtfully. "Fortunately, I keep anything related to our activities safely stowed away. Away from sticky fingers." She removed her satchel from the back of her chair and began to rummage around in it, finally pulling out a letter in triumph. "I knew better than to let this letter out of my sight. I did anticipate someone might search my room."

"When did you receive that?" said Fina. She could hear the rising irritation in her own voice, but was powerless to stop it.

"Just yesterday, dear Feens," said Ruby. "I've had time to read it once or twice, but I still haven't figured out exactly what it means," she said, handing the letter to Wendell. "Would you read it aloud, Wendy?"

"Certainly," he said, clearing his throat. His eyebrows rose when he looked at the envelope. "I see this is from Ian Clavering." He gave Ruby a wink.

"Don't be beastly, Wendy. This is serious," she said, her

mouth set in a grim line. It slowly gave way to a ghost of a smile. "Go on."

Dear Ruby,

I hope my last postcard reached you. As transatlantic mail can sometimes be unreliable, I thought it best to write you a letter as well.

Nassau is my home for a few more weeks. As beautiful and comfortable as it is, I am anxious to return to London to see you. I am so like my mother. She always says sheep do not give birth to goats, and that is certainly true. I cannot stay in one place too long.

During my travels, I've also thought a great deal about another saying – this time from my older sister. I love her dearly, but sometimes she is so serious! She says: "What is a joke to butchers is most certainly death to animals." Rather grim, but so true. When I try to laugh off much of what I see, it chips away at my soul.

But enough of that! I wrote to tell you how much I miss you, though I don't know when I will be in London again. I expect you are busy with papers and the like. And, knowing you, you will also be involved in some sort of escapade by this time. Do be careful, dear one.

Yours ever,
Ian

Wendell handed the letter to Fina for closer inspection. "So tell us what this missive means, great Detective Dove," said Wendell, leaning back in his chair and folding his arms behind his head.

Ruby smoothed her hair and skirt. "Well, I believe this is a more detailed warning than the one we received earlier. Ian wrote about the identity of the person watching us, or wrote more about the nature of the danger."

"Which one do you think it is – or is it both?" asked Fina.

"My intuition tells me it is about the identity rather than the nature of the danger. I'm not sure why I believe that, but it seems safer than revealing what is going on," Ruby said, taking a sip of her tea. "Besides, if he told us about the operation, but not the identity of the person spying on us, it wouldn't do us much good. All it would do is make us more worried than we are now."

Wendell nodded. "That rings true to me. Have you figured out the code yet?"

She shook her head. "I was hoping you might help us with that. It is your area of expertise."

Fina returned the letter to Wendell. She couldn't make head or tail of it. His eyes scrunched together. Fina noticed the slightest protrusion of his tongue out of the side of his mouth.

"Hmmm ... I think it must have something to do with one of the two proverbs in the letter."

"Yes, I thought of that," said Ruby. "Especially because Ian is definitely not one to recite proverbs. I've never heard him use one before."

Wendell read aloud: "Sheep do not give birth to goats – and – what is a joke to butchers is most certainly death to animals."

"Well, I must confess I feel like piffy on a rock bun with the two of you," said Fina. "But what about the first proverb? Could it be something related to a wolf in sheep's clothing?"

"You are most certainly not piffy on a rock bun, Feens," said Ruby in lightly scolding voice. "And I think it is a plausible idea ... thought I'm not sure how it tells us *who* is the wolf in sheep's clothing."

Ruby took the paper from Wendell and scrutinised it further. "The butcher language is grim and violent. Very unlike Ian. It must mean something."

"If we take the first two letters of each word, we end up with 'shdonogibitogo' and 'whisajotobuisdetoan,'" said Wendell, taking the letter back from Ruby. "And if we take just the first letter of each word, we end up with 'sdngbtg' and 'wiajtbidta'," he said, shaking his head. "May I make a copy of this, Ruby? I'd like to have it with me so I can think about it."

Ruby slid her hand into her satchel again and pulled out two carbon papers. "One for each of you," she said, as if she were a mother carefully handing out sweets to two competitive siblings.

Breakfast had been delicious and invigorating, but as soon as the three of them stepped out of the café, Fina felt exhausted. Her feet moved as if she were walking through a hulking vat of treacle.

"Ruby, I don't think I'll make it to the lecture with Bathurst. I need a nap."

Ruby consulted her watch. "You're right. I'm all in myself. It's 9:30. If we're lucky, we can catch Bathurst before he enters class, since he's almost always late. I want to ask him a few questions. Then we can both get at least an hour's sleep before we need to be at that luncheon."

"But won't you have to go to the lecture if you see him?" asked Fina.

"No, I'll tell him I have to prepare to meet with the police – a justified absence if ever there was one."

Wendell leaned back and stretched himself out, like a cat bathing in a pool of sunlight. Then he rubbed his hands together. "Right. I'm glad you two will get a little rest. Pixley and I are going to walk around Oxford a bit, but stay close to the Peacock and Parrot. Hogston said he wants me to be available for contact. I think he believes I control you two."

"And he is sadly misinformed," said Ruby.

33

"Now!" hissed Fina.

Ruby and Fina ambushed Professor Bathurst from behind opposite hedges as he bounded up the steps to the lecture hall. It seemed drastic, but Ruby had pointed out Bathurst would surely do anything to avoid them, especially after Vera's murder and the assault in the quad.

"Professor Bathurst," said Ruby as she approached him. He turned his head to the right, towards her. Then he turned his head to the left, as Fina approached him.

Aha, thought Fina. No escape.

"Ah, good morning Miss Dove, Miss Aubrey-Havelock. I'm afraid I'll have to dash as I'm late to lecture."

"Professor Bathurst, I'm sure you'll want to hear us out before the police arrive." As per usual, Ruby's flair for the dramatic had its effect.

Bathurst stood very still in a wide stance.

"We wanted to let you know the police have found the missing documents."

He gave them a smile. A forced smile. "Well, that's splendid.

Hopefully they can solve the murder now." He gulped. Fina watched his Adam's apple glide down his throat.

"I'm sure I don't have to tell you where they found those documents," said Ruby.

"I'm afraid I'm in the dark, Miss Dove," he said, licking his lips and patting down his hair.

"I'm afraid you're not. The secret room in the chemistry laboratory?"

He blinked. His arms dropped to his sides.

"I don't know what you're talking about," he said.

"Do you remember the day you showed us around the laboratory? You gave keys to each of a few senior students. I was one of them. At one particular moment, I remember you hesitated. And then you became excited. I think you wanted to show off to us a bit. You told us there was a secret storeroom. You called it a water closet, oddly enough. At the time, I was quite puzzled. I asked you why it was there, and you said it was something the builders added after they had finished the room. It was a bit of unused space, so they decided to make it into an additional large closet. Then, when Fina and I went poking around in the closet, she discovered a combination padlock behind an oil painting. At first, I tried your office number, but then I thought back to the water closet remark. And I tried the molecular combination of water. Presto."

"So what?" He stood up and loomed over Ruby, which was no small feat given her height – especially in heels.

"So what this means is we found the documents, including items Vera most likely stole, in that room. Your ... relationship with Vera is going to make this situation rather awkward for you when the police arrive."

The blustering, aggressive body posture vanished.

"Why are you telling me this? Why not let the police tell me?"

"Because in spite of how you treated me, Professor Bathurst, I believe you deserve a little time to think about how to defend yourself," said Ruby, quietly.

As they turned to leave the befuddled professor behind them, Ruby added, "And, because if I need a favour, I'm sure I can count on you."

They glided down the steps in triumph. Ruby said, "Let's see the *other* professor now."

Fina paused as they climbed up the steps to the hall where Professor Marlston's rooms were located. "Do you think she'll tell us anything?" she asked Ruby.

"No, but I'm hoping that talking to her will reveal something – I have a feeling she might say something which will at least make my little grey cells activate."

As they entered the hall, Fina noticed the leaves on the Virginia creeper were beginning to shrivel. The daylight no longer provided a warm glow but rather the anaemic filtered light of an approaching winter. She shivered and pulled up her collar.

As Fina prepared to knock on Professor Marlston's door, she halted. Voices from inside suggested she was busy with another student or professor.

Looking up and down the corridor, Ruby put her ear to the door and signalled to Fina to do the same.

"I'm not sure there's much to be done at this point," they heard Victoria say.

"Do you think I ought to tell the police?"

The second voice was James.

There was a distinct pause. "I cannot see what relevance it has now. If you tell them, it will only draw suspicion to you," said Victoria.

"But surely they wouldn't think it was enough of a reason for murder."

Another pause.

"You came to me for advice, and I say you keep this to yourself. I'll do the same," said Victoria.

The shuffling of papers and feet indicated they should move away from the door.

James exited, head down, looking more than ever like a forlorn puppy with his hair hanging over his eyes.

"James!" said Fina in an overly casual voice.

He spun round, nearly dropping his briefcase as he was wont to do.

"Were you talking to Marlston about the term paper for our French history course?"

He blinked. Then he recovered.

"Oh, ah, yes. I wanted to talk to her about possibly pursuing a theme of France-New Zealand relationships."

"I see. Is there a relationship?"

"Oh yes. The two countries were quite close in the Great War," he said, rubbing his forehead as if he could predict historical events rather than the future.

Fina had to admit she had underestimated James. Perhaps there was more to him than met the eye?

Ruby tried another tack. "I'm so sorry about Vera. I know you were fond of her."

Tears welled up. He wiped them away quickly.

"Yes, I am rather upset," he said, edging away as if this provided a convenient excuse for him to leave the interrogation. "Good to see you both," he mumbled. He scurried off, but not before he dropped his briefcase again.

"That man will make an excellent absent-minded professor," said Fina. Then she turned and whispered, even though the corridor was empty: "What do you think that was all about? Was James asking if he ought to reveal his infatuation with Vera?"

"It could be," said Ruby, "though he's also infatuated with Gayatri. It does seem the most plausible explanation..."

Footsteps interrupted their conversation. Victoria's head popped out of the open doorway.

"May I help you two? Fina – are you here to talk about the class?"

"We came to see if you were all right. After last night. And we'd like to talk to you about the murders, to be honest," said Fina. She could sense Ruby's body tightening next to her. But surely the direct route would be the best. After all, Victoria was someone who was rather blunt herself.

Though her eyes narrowed, Victoria said, "Come in, both of you."

They entered Professor Marlston's room. It was packed with books, floor to ceiling. They were arranged by height on each shelf. Victoria had an impressive collection of tomes, even for a professor. One lonesome spider plant sat in the corner. Fina saw an open box of papers, arranged in alphabetical order. Unlike the other offices, where one could easily become asthmatic just by breathing, nary a speck of dust could be seen by the naked eye.

Fina peered at the professor more closely. Her curly blonde hair was tidy and her eyes did not hold the tell-tale signs of sleeplessness. But she walked stiffly, as if last night's altercation had left its marks. Plus, her face was more puffy than usual, with little broken capillaries beginning to emerge on her nose. Was she hitting the bottle more regularly? It might have nothing to do with the murders, Fina thought. The politics of the university would be enough to drive anyone to drink.

There was only one truly personal item in the room. Next to the spider plant sat a large framed photograph of a small child and a woman sitting in a rowing boat. From the dress and hairstyles, it looked to be perhaps fifteen to twenty years old.

Fina tried her hand at small talk to soften her up. "Is that you in the photograph – when you were a child?"

Victoria craned to look over her shoulder.

"Yes, that's me and my mother. We were boating on the River Mersey."

Turning back, Victoria cleared her throat as if to signal it was time to get down to business. So much for small talk. "In answer to your questions, I'm perfectly well, thank you. It was an unpleasant incident, based on vile prejudices that are not, unfortunately, so very uncommon in this cloistered community." She raised a well-groomed eyebrow at the pair and waited.

Fina repressed the urge to giggle. So that's what the professor thought of herself and Ruby. Well, if it induced her to open up to them, in a rush of fellow-feeling, then so much the better.

"I'm so glad to hear you're not hurt," said Ruby, maintaining her composure with some effort. "Do you mind if we ask a few questions?"

"Of course not. How can I help you?" Victoria squared off a stack of papers on her desk.

"We were wondering first if you think the theft of Mr Gasthorpe's papers is somehow tied to these murders," said Fina as her opening gambit.

"Papers? What papers?"

"Surely you must know. They were stolen from his rooms the day after the murder. Jack Devenish has been very worried about it, I believe."

Victoria leaned back and then leaned forward to continue squaring off the already perfectly aligned stack of paper. "No, I don't believe I know about this."

"No doubt the police will tell you about it in time," said Ruby.

"No doubt," replied Victoria. "But given everything that

happened the other night, as well as the murders, I'm not getting involved with the police over some thefts which have nothing to do with me." Was she afraid her relationship with Grace might land her in hot water if the police got to know about it, wondered Fina? Or was there something specifically in those papers she wanted to keep hush hush?

The door opened, saving Victoria from having to answer anything further.

"Vicky. Oh," said Grace, waltzing in as if it were her own office. She wore a chartreuse blouse and black trousers. Seeing Fina and Ruby, she halted and awkwardly backed out of the room like a crab. "I see you're engaged – I'll come back later."

"No, no, Miss Yingxia," said Ruby, rising out of her seat. "We were just leaving."

The pair said their goodbyes and walked out, but Ruby stopped in the corridor and winked at Fina. She had that look on her face which meant she was about to put a plan into action. Fina caught her breath. Perhaps this would be the moment when, with one skewering question or icily logical deduction, Ruby broke the case wide open.

Through the open doorway, Ruby called out to the two women in the office: "Do either of you wear eyeglasses, or have trouble with your eyes?"

34

"Selkies and kelpies!" said Fina as they made their way out into the quad. "What do eyeglasses have to do with the case?"

"I wanted to see how they would react to a sudden, seemingly odd, question," said Ruby.

"Hmmm ... I know you, Miss Ruby Dove, and there must be more to it than that."

"Perhaps. But I do know neither of them apparently wears eyeglasses." Changing the subject, Ruby said, "I suppose we have to go this luncheon. It's almost noon."

"Thank goodness, I'm ravenous," said Fina. "Where is it going to be held?"

"At Trafford College. I asked Beatrice about it this morning. She said we couldn't have it in the college dining room since that will be in use by everyone. I think she'd prefer not to draw any more prying eyes to a gathering of the suspects."

"Is that what it is? A gathering of suspects?"

"Well, that's not what it's called. I think the dean feels terribly obligated to play host as long as so many people have to remain in Oxford," said Ruby as they turned onto the Banbury

Road. "Pixley and Wendell said they'd be waiting for us outside the Peacock and Parrot so we can all walk over together."

Soon they could see the tall figure of Wendell and the short figure of Pixley standing underneath the carved sign of the inn. Pixley sported high-waisted tweed trousers with a striped tie. His fedora was tipped at an angle, completing the jaunty, relaxed look. Wendell, on the other hand, wore a serious navy suit. Fina noticed Argyle socks peeking out, however, when he moved toward them.

Ruby and Fina exchanged air kisses this time with both of them, instead of hugs. Hugs seemed only appropriate when they hadn't seen someone for at least a day.

Fina fell into step with Pixley as Ruby and Wendell spoke in hushed tones in front of them.

"How are you getting on? It must be terrible for a journalist to have to wait so long in one place," said Fina, sympathetically.

Pixley grimaced. "Yes, it is rather bothersome, but I have caught up on a great deal of correspondence. And it has been jolly good to see Wendell."

They turned onto a narrow alley to take a shortcut to Trafford College. Fina caught the smell of chips coming from one of the kitchens facing onto the alley. Her stomach rumbled.

"Do you have any theories about what happened – in the case of Vera's murder?"

He shook his head. "No, but Wendell was able to find out from the police this morning something most interesting – at least for me."

Fina shook her head in awe. "It's quite amazing they give Wendell information simply because he's a Navy lieutenant."

"Yes," said Pixley thoughtfully. "I certainly did not receive that treatment." He turned his head to one side and said, "But back to my story. You see, I've always suspected Gasthorpe of some rather dirty dealings in the journalism department, as I hinted before."

"Do you mean you have more information about those dirty dealings now?"

He nodded. "What made me suspicious of him was his seemingly overnight transformation into a success. Last year, no one knew his name, and then within a week he became a darling of the public and news media – and that was even before he published his atrocious book."

"Why did that make you suspicious? I know a lot of people appear to have had overnight success, but they've actually been toiling away in obscurity for years," said Fina.

"Precisely," said Pixley. "That's what I assumed at first. But when I looked into his background – particularly his supposedly hardscrabble beginnings – I could find nothing at all, except that he was from a small, prosperous area near Liverpool. What was even more suspicious was that he was churning out articles at a rate which seemed nearly impossible. No one could write that fast, let alone produce that many ideas. These weren't even strictly news stories, but more opinion-essay type pieces."

"So you did some research initially and found..."

"After I looked through all the stories he had published in the past year, I came across one that struck me as familiar. And then it hit me. It was my essay!"

Fina's eyes widened. "Plagiarism?"

"Exactly. Mind you, he had changed enough in the story to make it look like his own. He took the research content – about European colonial interests in Africa – and then gave it his own take on the issue, which was, of course, completely different to mine."

"So what you're saying is he took other people's stories, stole the content, and then essentially wrote his own introduction and conclusion paragraphs?"

Pixley nodded eagerly. "He targeted journalists whose politics differed from his, so they were unlikely to come across his features. He also chose work by journalists who were relatively obscure. I was that way myself until recently," he said with a smile.

"So how did the police confirm your suspicions?"

"Well, they're still sorting through those masses of papers you and Ruby discovered last night – excellent sleuthing, by the way – and told Wendell to ask me to come to the station. They found a stack of articles of mine among the papers. The scribbled notes attached to them looked like a first attempt at rewriting my story to be his own. I suppose they wanted to see my reaction to the news. I told them it confirmed what I had thought, and they let me go. I think they realised it wasn't enough to pin the murder on me – it's not enough of a reason to kill someone. It would have been more satisfying for me, at least, to expose him as a fraud."

"What are you going to do about it?"

They turned onto the pathway leading to the main quad. It was a small pathway, so they had to walk single-file.

Fina turned her head behind her to hear what Pixley had to say.

But he had vanished into the ether.

Fina spun around in a full circle. She repeated the motion and then felt quite dizzy.

"Stop!" she yelled at Wendell and Ruby as they traipsed along, lost in conversation.

They turned together and began to trot back toward Fina.

"What's the matter? Where's Pixley?" asked Ruby.

"That's just it. He's vanished," said Fina, throwing up her hands. "We were talking about Gasthorpe's plagiarism of his news story. We came to this little pathway where we had to move single-file. I turned round to finish our conversation and he was gone."

Wendell chuckled. "I know it must seem peculiar," he said. "But when Pixley sees something or someone who makes him think of a story, he dashes off without so much as a word. I remember once in Grenada when he saw a local politician he knew would be up on corruption charges. He scampered off without even looking back at me. Fortunately, I saw him do it so at least I knew where he had gone."

"Should we wait for him before we go in?" asked Ruby.

Wendell rubbed his chin thoughtfully. "No, I think he'll make his way when he's ready. I expect he'll catch us up."

"Won't he have trouble finding us?" queried Fina.

"You forget, the man is a journalist," said Wendell, looking up at the sky. The sunny day was gone and the clouds were rolling in as quickly as a March louse.

Ruby shivered. "I felt a raindrop on my nose. Let's hurry to the hall."

35

The smells of fried aubergine and pork pie wafted from the dining room as they entered. Fina looked to her left. She saw Enid, James, and Gayatri at one table. James sipped his water, staring vacantly at a blank wall. Gayatri looked in high spirits, dunking large chunks of bread into tomato soup. After sopping up the liquid, she lodged the bread in her mouth with great gusto. In contrast, Enid's eyes were red. She ate the beans on her plate methodically and mechanically, one by one.

To her right, Fina saw Ossie, Grace, Victoria, and Esmond sitting at another round table with a blue linen tablecloth. Dean Ossington had apparently had quite an appetite, as her plate was already empty. She made conversation with Grace, but Fina could tell from the frequency with which the dean twirled her pearl necklace that all was not well. Grace appeared relaxed – almost sleepy. She would take one minuscule bite of her salad and then set the fork down as if she were finished. Professors Marlston and Bathurst, meanwhile, looked appalled to be sitting next to one another. They did not look up from their plates. One might think they were engaged in an eating contest given the rapidity of their bites and the attention they gave to their meals.

Beatrice hovered near Dean Ossington, swaying back and forth as if there were music playing in the background. She nodded to Wendell, Ruby and Fina when they moved towards the table with the students. The three sat down and made themselves comfortable. Within a few minutes, Beatrice had brought them steaming bowls of tomato soup.

"May I have some more rolls, please, Beatrice?" gambled Fina.

"Of course, miss. I'll fetch them now."

In an uncharacteristic opening move, Ruby began to gossip with everyone at the table. "Did you hear? It turns out Harold Baden Gasthorpe wasn't such a superstar journalist after all. He plagiarised his articles!"

At that, James choked on his bread. He began to make a great gasping sound. Wendell rose rapidly and began to bang on James's back. The blockage popped out onto the table. Fortunately for the appetites of everyone else, he draped his napkin over it before anyone could see it.

"Are you all right, James?" asked Wendell as he bent over the tall man.

James waved his hand. "Yes," he said weakly. Looking up at Wendell, he said, "Thanks, old man. Don't know what happened."

Now that a crisis had been averted, Gayatri said, "You mean he stole other journalists' stories?"

Ruby nodded. "Could be quite a good motive for murder."

"For a journalist," said Gayatri. She craned her neck around the room. "Speaking of which, where is Mr Hayford? And for that matter, Mr Devenish?"

As if on cue, both men strode into the dining room, one after another. Jack wore a rather loud striped suit with a fedora. When he removed his hat, Fina saw his hair was dirty and dishevelled. The glory of his suit was diminished by its crumpled state. Pixley ran his hand over the top of his smooth head. In an obviously unintentional comic gesture, both men looked at each other and then quickly looked away. Jack moved toward the dean's table, while Pixley naturally gravitated toward Wendell.

Once seated, Pixley drank an entire glass of water without stopping and then wiped his forehead with a handkerchief.

"Where did you vanish to, Pixley?" enquired Ruby.

"I'm so sorry – particularly to Fina – but I saw Jack Devenish out of the corner of my eye when we were near the entrance to the college. I had to confront him while I had the chance to get him alone."

"And what did he have to say for himself?" enquired Wendell. "Did he know about the plagiarism?"

"He claims he figured it out about a month ago, but decided it wasn't his place to do anything about it," said Pixley with a snort. "What kind of world is this? Have people no ethics anymore?"

"I'm afraid not," said Enid vehemently. It was as if she had awoken from a stupor. "The world is a wicked, wicked place. People are tricked into doing things they'd not do otherwise – if their minds weren't muddled."

"I disagree," said James, thumping his water glass on the table. "I believe people are fully in control of their choices and their destiny. There are many obstacles, of course, but that's no excuse to lose one's moral compass." He was warming to the subject as if they were preparing for an academic debate.

Pixley jumped in. "I come down on the issue somewhere in between you two," he said, waving his fork about. Fina thought he looked almost delirious. His forehead was sweating and his eyes looked glassy. "People are basically decent creatures, but there are all kinds of structures that make us do horrible things, sometimes. It's not that we've lost our moral compass, but that morality is in the eye of the beholder."

They were saved from further pronouncements on this topic by the entry of Chief Inspector Hogston, Constable Clumber, and Detective Sergeant Snorscomb. Looking solemn, they marched in, nodded at the dean and then took seats at a central, empty table.

Dean Ossington rose from her table to address the gathering. She cleared her throat.

"I appreciate you all traipsing over from Quenby to come to this luncheon. I also apologise for not informing you the police would be joining us," she said with a surprisingly dismissive wave in their direction.

Everyone shifted in their seats. They all jumped when a piece of silverware hit one of the dishes. Wendell hurriedly put away a notebook he'd been scribbling in.

The dean continued. "The police have informed me they are ready to make an arrest..." she said, starting off loudly but ending with a whimper as she took her seat.

Out of the corner of her eye, Fina could perceive a multitude of heads whipping around to exchange glances with their neighbours. She herself gave Ruby a look of genuine surprise. Fina leaned over and whispered, "Did you know this was going to happen?"

Ruby shook her head, absently. Her brain was already on overdrive.

"What are we going to do?" whispered Fina again.

"Play along." Ruby paused and patted Fina's arm. "Don't worry."

"Please, Miss Aubrey-Havelock. We need silence," said Hogston, as if she were still in primary school. Fina's body reacted predictably to the accusation. Those warm pinpricks of embarrassment crept up her neck once again.

Hogston removed his trench coat and homburg. He had on the same suit as the first night. Small wonder, thought Fina. The man probably hasn't slept for three days. Snorscomb and Clumber sat erect, flanking Hogston on each side, scanning the faces of everyone in the room.

"Thank you, Dean Ossington. Yes, we've gathered you all here today to explain what happened in these crimes. And to make an arrest," he said, nodding at Clumber who immediately popped up and flew to the door in his cape. He stood sentry without moving a muscle, as if he were guarding Buckingham Palace.

"I demand to speak to a solicitor!" said Professor Bathurst, leaping up from his seat.

Hogston made a little calming gesture with his hands that also told Bathurst to retake his seat. "There will be time enough for that later, Professor Bathurst. We're just going to have a little discussion amongst ourselves. It's much easier to tie up some loose ends with everyone in the room."

Then he stepped aside, as if he were introducing his co-star in the production. He pointed at Snorscomb. "I've asked the Detective Sergeant here to start us off."

Standing up a little too quickly, Snorscomb nearly knocked over his chair. He readjusted his brown tie a few times.

"Thank you, Chief Inspector," he said, his voice cracking. "I'd like to recount the events of the first murder."

"Get on with it, man," snapped Esmond, as if he were a heckler preparing to throw some not-so-fresh produce at the stage.

Hogston rose in a masculine challenge to Esmond. Oh Lord, thought Fina.

Esmond pursed his lips, but kept the look of defiance on his face.

At last Snorscomb found the courage to leave his tie alone

and continue his speech. "That first night, the night of the murder, Mr Gasthorpe gave the annual Luffnum lecture. All the guests here were in attendance."

"Tell us something we don't know," said Esmond.

After a look from Hogston, Clumber began to advance on Esmond.

"If you don't pipe down, we'll have to remove you," said Hogston.

Bathurst put up his hands in mock surrender.

Clearly unnerved by the outbursts, Snorscomb continued somewhat shakily. "After the lecture, Dean Ossington hosted a sherry party for the honoured guests. All of you were present, plus a number of other attendees. At approximately nine o'clock, Fina Aubrey-Havelock had a confrontation with the deceased in which she assaulted Mr Gasthorpe. Mr Gasthorpe fell onto the floor, backwards, as a result of this physical assault.

Fina felt ashamed, yet again. But she could see a curve of a smile on Ruby's face.

"Fortunately for Miss Aubrey-Havelock, the autopsy confirmed Gasthorpe did not die due to any trauma to the head. The autopsy did confirm, however, that the deceased died from acute poisoning by means of liquid nicotine. We also confirmed that when Gasthorpe died at 9:30, the nicotine had been administered approximately fifteen minutes before that. In between the assault and his death, we know Gasthorpe left the room to visit the, er, conveniences. We also know, from Mr Devenish's testimony, that Gasthorpe's pipe had been emptied during the assault – as a result of it falling to the floor – but when Gasthorpe returned, he had resumed smoking."

"So the pipe tobacco was poisoned. Isn't that what you're saying?" Victoria suggested.

Snorscomb nodded. "Yes, Professor Marlston. The autopsy ruled out the food being contaminated with nicotine. It also confirmed it could have been in the sherry, but we doubt that was the vehicle, for two reasons. First, the sherry was shared by everyone, in glasses, so it would be extremely difficult to predict which glass would reach Mr Gasthorpe. Second, while we suppose a glass could have been cleaned – though it seems like a logistical nightmare to do so – we did not find any traces of nicotine in any of the glasses. Neither did we find liquid residue anywhere on his lips or in his throat."

"What do you conclude, then?" asked Grace. "That the pipe tobacco was contaminated and he inhaled the nicotine?"

Snorscomb nodded. "That is indeed the most likely explanation, Miss Yingxia. When concentrated nicotine is inhaled, death occurs quite rapidly. Unfortunately for us, the tobacco tin was empty. The murderer was careful to make sure there would be just enough tobacco left for one pipeful."

"Was there residue on the pipe or in the tin?" queried Enid.

The detective sergeant shook his head. "There was nicotine residue, of course, but that's to be expected. No, the murderer prepared the tobacco ahead of time so it could absorb the liquid. Otherwise, Gasthorpe would have thought it odd that his tobacco was wet – and would have most likely discarded it."

Heads bobbed in understanding around the room.

"So this leads us to the conclusion that one – or possibly two – of you in this room committed the murder," said Snorscomb on an ominous note. He was enjoying this role a bit too much, thought Fina.

Hogston popped up and nodded thanks to Snorscomb, who took his seat.

"What do we know about the deceased?" began Hogston. "We all know he was a journalist and essayist who had a big breakthrough success with his book. He was prolific and had an eye on most likely entering the political arena, perhaps standing for parliament. His politics were—"

Fina couldn't help herself. "Vile, Chief Inspector. Absolutely the most atrocious claptrap I've ever heard."

Ruby put a calming but warning hand on Fina.

"But he was a most vociferous advocate of women's rights, and of aid to the poor," said Dean Ossington.

"Please," said Hogston. "We're not here to discuss the merits of his political views. We're here to establish what possible motive people had to murder him," he said with finality.

"Now, to continue." He shifted his weight from side to side. "Gasthorpe's rise to the top was surprisingly quick, especially given the fact he grew up in poverty. We also know he was prepared to give Quenby College a large sum of money, most likely the night he died."

"How did he become famous so rapidly?" asked Grace, clearly not without a self-interested perspective. Perhaps a moderately successful poet could follow his lead.

"Well, according to our sources, as well as the papers we found yesterday, thanks to the efforts of Miss Dove and Miss Aubrey-Havelock," Hogston said with a grudging look of gratitude in their direction, "it looks as though Mr Gasthorpe was involved in many illegal and unethical practices."

"I can tell you one," said Pixley, looking venomously at Jack Devenish. "He plagiarised other journalists' stories and passed them off as his own."

"That's right, Mr Hayford," said Hogston, suddenly snapping out of his lackadaisical pose. "And you had a motive to seek revenge."

Although Pixley already looked feverish, he was remarkably calm. "Hardly, my dear Chief Inspector. It's true I suspected as much, and in fact I came here to look into his activities, but I had no proof. I couldn't murder a man because he stole a story from me. It would have been better to expose him as a fraud."

"Be that as it may, it still gives you a motive," said Snorscomb from behind Hogston.

Pixley shrugged.

"We also know Gasthorpe's dodgy practices created another reason for someone to kill him. As a journalist, particularly one who was unethical, he came into certain types of damaging knowledge about various people's affairs. Now, strictly speaking, Gasthorpe did not engage in extortion – as far as we know – but nevertheless he had certain documents he held onto. He did not expect money in return."

"I think it gave him a sense of security to have dirt on other people, especially because he was so dirty himself," said Jack.

Hogston spun round. "Quite right, Mr Devenish. And we know a few people implicated in those stories are here. But the real question is: why didn't you tell anyone, or leave his employ? After all, he wasn't an easy man to work with. We understand he cycled through secretaries quite quickly."

Like Pixley, Jack shrugged. "The money was good. And to be honest, Chief Inspector, I've never met a businessman who strictly abided by ethical principles yet."

Ruby looked like she was about to speak. But then she leaned back in her chair, apparently thinking it over.

"What about the other suspects, Chief Inspector?" Wendell demanded, also noticing Ruby's indecision.

"Ah yes. Let's start with the students, shall we?" He turned toward their table. "Enid Wiverton had no ostensible reason to commit this crime, though we will come back to her for the second murder. James Matua has been known to express extremist political views, in opposition to Mr Gasthorpe. Some young hotheads these days have no objection to carrying out assassinations of public figures they find objectionable. Mr Matua also had a motive for the second crime, which we'll come to later. And Ruby Dove – she also had a political motive, but no apparent motive strong enough to provoke murder."

Then his eyes rested on Fina. "Fina Aubrey-Havelock is a different kettle of fish."

"Miss Aubrey-Havelock is not a kettle of fish, *Chief Inspector*," said Ruby with a steely voice.

Fina gave her a grateful smile. "Yes, Chief Inspector?"

"Your family went through quite a scandal, didn't it?"

Fina's hands balled into little fists.

"I'm well aware Gasthorpe used my case to bolster his anti-Irish propaganda. He apparently had some more information about the case, but I have no idea what it was."

"You have the strongest motive of anyone here, which is pure hatred and revenge," said Hogston quietly.

Ruby stood up suddenly. "Chief Inspector. If Miss Aubrey-Havelock wanted revenge on Gasthorpe, why would she draw attention to herself in such a public way by assaulting him – and then coldly calculate a murder at the same time? It doesn't make any sense, and you know it."

"But couldn't she have planned it that way? A sort of double ruse?" asked Devenish from the other side of the room.

"Yes," chimed in Enid. Fina looked over at her in surprise. "Ruby could have given her the nicotine, since she's a chemistry student. Then she could have planned the assault to draw attention away from herself."

A strange sense of calm washed over Fina. She had never experienced this feeling. She stood up and said quietly, "Well if it was a double ruse, it apparently didn't work." She held her arms out together to Hogston in a theatrical gesture. "Arrest me if you're so confident."

Hogston turned a little pink, like his namesake. "No, Miss Aubrey-Havelock. I do not have enough evidence to arrest you ... yet."

Fina sat back down, feeling satisfied. However, the sight of Enid next to her now made her skin crawl. Enid had to be the one sent to spy on them. This change in her personality – if it was one – showed she was covering something.

Hogston left their table and ambled over to what Fina thought of as the "serious adult" table. Everyone there turned their necks to get a good look at the officer.

"Professor Marlston and Grace Yingxia," he said simply, adjusting his hat at a slight angle.

The two swished their bobbed heads at one another. "Yes?" they said in unison.

"Isn't it true Mr Gasthorpe had some information about your relationship you would rather have had kept secret?"

Fina could see Grace's back stiffen, but she kept her hands in her lap.

"What do you mean, exactly, Chief Inspector?" demanded Victoria as if she were asking a student to explain an incoherent answer.

"I mean that you two are in a, ah, relationship ... of an intimate nature with one another."

The pair gave each other a quick glance. Victoria nodded at Grace.

Grace said, "I don't see any point in denying it, although I cannot see what Gasthorpe has to do with this."

"In his papers, we found letters between the two of you in which you call each other 'darling' and quite a few more terms of affection," he said sheepishly. Then he cleared his throat. "We also have independent confirmation from others who have overheard you in conversation."

Fina thought the two were taking this rather calmly.

Out of the corner of her eye, she saw Ruby flinch.

"I assure you, Chief Inspector, we did not know he had such letters, so there really is no motive for us to have committed the murder."

"Aside from that," chimed in Victoria, "how would we secure liquid nicotine? Neither of us is involved in chemistry and I didn't even know nicotine existed in liquid form before this case."

"Ah yes, chemistry," said Hogston, seizing this segue to the next victim. "Professor Bathurst, professor of chemistry. Who runs a laboratory..." He turned to Esmond.

Esmond sat slumped in his chair, arms across his chest.

"Not only does this cast a suspicious light on Professor Bathurst for the first murder, but it also implicates him in the second."

Esmond said nothing. Then he slid forward on his chair and slapped his thighs. "Could you speak plainly, Chief Inspector? I'm afraid I'm not following your line of thought."

"But Vera Sapperton followed you all right. Didn't she?" Hogston's voice was suddenly menacing. "And it proved to be her undoing."

"Why, Chief Inspector," drawled Esmond, drawing out the words as though he was talking to a small child. "This is all a load of nonsense. Whatever you're implying, you've got not a jot of evidence, and you won't find any. I was nowhere near Vera that night, either when she died, or earlier that same evening."

"No, you weren't. You didn't need to be," said Hogston with a sneer. "And yet you killed her just as sure as I'm standing here. You're running a drug ring out of this college, Professor Bathurst."

36

While everyone else gasped, Fina let out a "selkies and kelpies" exclamation that temporarily drew everyone's attention away from Esmond.

Soon, however, silence enveloped the room once more.

Esmond began to laugh. He threw back his head and a great, evil cackle reverberated around the room.

"Drugs, Chief Inspector? I assume you mean nicotine. Or cocaine?" Though his cackle had abated, small burbling noises like giggles in his stomach occasionally escaped through his mouth.

Crack.

Jack Devenish's chair had fallen backwards as he rose from the table. "Chief Inspector, let me take a swing at him," he said, his American accent becoming more pronounced.

"You?" asked Hogston and Snorscomb.

Devenish pulled out his wallet, opened it and handed it over to Hogston. "I'm a detective in New York, over here to work with Customs and Excise," he said, turning toward the crowd. Fina swore his shoulders became squarer as soon as he announced his real profession.

He lit a cigarette, making an elaborate gesture of waving the match as it went out. "I was sent here to investigate a drug smuggling ring between New York and Southampton. We knew large quantities of cocaine were arriving via sea, but we had no idea who was running it and from where. We had a tip that Gasthorpe was somehow involved, though we couldn't tell at the time if he was implicated himself, or whether he was like me – investigating the ones running it. So I decided to apply for his open secretary position, and I got a whole lot more than I bargained for, as we all know. Gasthorpe was a real treat. A tyrant, a bully and a liar. But I stuck with it because I didn't have a choice. Besides, it wasn't like I was relying on him for a reference."

Fina looked over at Hogston and Snorscomb. Snorscomb's eyes were wide, as if he were in the presence of royalty. Hogston's drawn face was a mixture of exhaustion and resignation.

Devenish took a long drag on his cigarette and continued. "It was clear from the first that Gasthorpe was not a user of cocaine, which did make sense if he were involved at higher levels in the smuggling ring. After about a month, I recognized our distinct pattern of travel. At first, it seemed haphazard because we were travelling from one end of the country to another. But then I began to realise that every few weeks he'd be solicited to speak at a university. What struck me as odd – besides the pattern itself – was that these talks seemed, well, kind of below him in terms of his nose for publicity. He was always trying to get more and more prestigious speaking venues, so going to give a talk at a small college at the University of Liverpool, for example, seemed like a step down in the world."

Devenish snapped his fingers. "Then I got it. Gasthorpe was the contact person – quite possibly the boss, as we'd say in the States – for the smuggling ring. That meant the cocaine was being distributed to universities. At first, I tried to figure out which students he met with. I confronted Vera about it one night, but she denied she had anything to do with processing it in the lab, or distributing it to the students. And then it hit me."

"It was the professors," said Ruby, quietly.

Devenish pointed at Ruby with a smile. "You're so right, Miss Dove. The professors! Brilliant. And it wasn't only that they were professors. They were professors of science, most often of—"

"Chemistry!" said Snorscomb, as if he had just won a competition.

All eyes in the room slid toward Esmond's chair. His face had aged at least ten years. He sat calmly, immobile apart from the keys he was jingling in his pocket.

Despite the visible strain he was under, Esmond said, quite confidently, "You've no proof at all. Not a shred of evidence for these outrageous charges."

Devenish turned toward Hogston, lifting his chin with a slight nod.

Hogston stood up and cleared his throat. "We will return to the issue of evidence in a few moments, Professor Bathurst. Mr Devenish's revelations bring us to the important point in the second murder, which is drugs; specifically, cocaine."

Hogston moved like a tiger toward the students' table.

"Who had a reason to kill Vera Sapperton? Unlike the first murder, there were quite a few student motives. Dismissing Mr Hayford for a moment, as he had no ostensible motive at all, we come to Miss Wiverton, Mr Matua, Miss Badarur, Miss Dove, and Miss Aubrey-Havelock."

They all cast their eyes downward as if various items on the table had become irresistibly fascinating.

"Miss Wiverton," he said. Enid's eyes flashed and she held her head high. For once, thought Fina.

"You were close friends with Vera. Very close. So close you thought her attention to Professor Bathurst was competing with your own time with her. You must have suspected she was also taking more time to herself because of something else. Because of the cocaine. You killed her in a fit of jealous rage, didn't you, Miss Wiverton?"

Fina looked over at Ruby. She was highly trained now in detecting the near-imperceptible sighs of disgust or resignation from Miss Ruby Dove. Undeniably, Hogston was clutching at straws.

"It's a lie, Chief Inspector! I didn't do it. I cared for Vera – I wouldn't harm her."

Hogston, saying nothing, slid his eyes toward James. "And you, young man, were not only in love with her – and therefore jealous of Bathurst – but also suspected her of stealing one of your papers." James looked accusingly at Victoria. Without thinking, he fumbled for a sheet of paper in his bag and began to tear it into perfectly circular scraps.

Tears welled up in his eyes. "I couldn't harm her – or anyone, for that matter. I don't know where you got the idea I was in love with her. There's someone else," he said, barely moving his eyes in the direction of Gayatri.

He wiped away his tears. "And yes, she did plagiarise my paper. If things had been different, I might have gone to the college authorities about it. But I would hardly have killed her over it, Chief Inspector!" Furtively, he put his hand to his mouth and popped in the scrap of paper, clearly hoping everyone would think he'd simply been clearing his throat.

Defeated once again, Hogston moved on to Gayatri. Gayatri was an old hand at this game. She held her head high and looked straight at Hogston. "Yes, Chief Inspector? I suppose it's my turn. I'll save you the trouble. I did suspect Vera stole my work in the laboratory as well. The bigger motive for me, however, was my worry about the college thief – and the possible connection to drugs. You see, I began to suspect Vera was the one who stole women's undergarments—"

A small gasp arose from those in the crowd who did not already know about the thief.

"– and other items. I saw the tell-tale signs of drug abuse in Vera. So I thought, quite logically, that she was stealing items to pay for her habit. I began to think the theft of women's undergarments was an elaborate ruse to make it look like the thief was, well, a little soft in the head. Or perhaps she hoped to plant the idea the culprit was a man. At any rate, after speaking to Dean Ossington about her own experience of the thefts, I began to realise some items Vera stole were quite valuable. That seemed to confirm she needed cash."

"That's why you were in the laboratory searching, wasn't it?" asked James. Apparently James had seen more that day than he'd let on.

Gayatri's eyebrows shot up in disbelief.

Hogston glared at Gayatri. "Out with it, Miss Badarur."

She cleared her throat and threw back her chest defiantly. "Well, yes. I didn't see the need to mention it at the time. It wasn't related to the murder. I had a suspicion Vera was the college thief so when I saw her leaving the halls of residence very quietly, as if she wished to remain unobserved, I followed her. She went to the laboratory. I watched her go into a closet in the laboratory with a full bag and then come out with an empty one. When I searched the closet, I found some of the items I knew were missing. I hid them away in my own wardrobe until I could think about what to do. I didn't want to get Vera in trouble, even though she was never kind to me. I could tell she had some reason to steal."

Esmond cleared his throat. Hogston spun round on his heel. "Yes, Professor Bathurst?"

"Vera was what I believe psychologists would term a kleptomaniac. She couldn't help herself. She stole everything she could get her hands on, including things like papers and assignments. I know she stole those papers from Gasthorpe and hid them in the closet in the lab. That may have been purely out of fear, after the murder. But it had nothing to do with needing cash for a drug habit, Chief Inspector."

"So you admit you had a relationship with her?"

Esmond began to grind his teeth. He said quietly, "Yes, I admit it. But it is completely unrelated to drugs."

Dean Ossington croaked, "Then who killed Vera?"

Ruby stood, turning in the direction of a figure standing in the corner. Beatrice.

"Miss Truelove, I think it's time to tell the truth, don't you? Before some innocent is sent to the gallows."

37

Sniff. Sniff.

They all turned toward Beatrice. She was wiping her eyes with the corner of her apron.

"Those drugs is evil," she said. "I'm glad I did what I did, so at least Professor Bathurst will stop his wicked ways. Preying on students like that. It's not right."

"Tell them what you did," said Ruby, urging her on.

"I– I– I, well, I found her dead, the night she died. You see, I knew the cocaine going round the college was no ordinary cocaine. I knew it was different. Super-concentrated, like the adverts say for those tinned soups, oxtail and the like. Something you might do in a laboratory," she said, looking venomously at Esmond.

"When I was doing my usual rounds at night, I saw something odd. Miss Vera's door was open, just a crack. I tapped at her door. No answer. I went in and I found her like we found her that morning," she said, waving toward Ruby and Fina.

James rose and found a chair for Beatrice. She smiled at him and sat down on the chair.

"I realised it was the cocaine. She had taken too much, the

poor lamb, or didn't count on it being that strong since it was this new, concentrated stuff. Seeing her laying there, all the life gone out of her, I was angry, uncommonly angry," she said, clearly reliving the moment as she clenched her jaw.

"I knew many students saw Vera as stuck-up. High and mighty. But in the short time I knew her, I saw her generous side. She noticed some holes in my dresses and insisted she buy me a new one. She always asked after my family, too."

Fina's stomach turned as she recalled all the terrible thoughts she'd had about Vera. But they were true, too.

Beatrice got up from her seat and began a pantomime of her actions after she had discovered the body. "So I went to the cellar, where we keep the rat poison," she said, walking as if she were creeping downstairs. "And then I mixed a bit of it into Miss Vera's silver snuff box with the cocaine. I thought I'd put enough in there to make it look like she was murdered on purpose. Because she *was* murdered, by the wicked one who gave her those drugs," she said, throwing daggers with her eyes at Esmond.

Esmond shook his head. "It wasn't me."

Beatrice continued, as if he hadn't spoken. "But then I was confused when the police said it was nicotine poisoning, like Mr Gasthorpe. But then I said to myself, Beatrice, what do you know about what's in rat poison, anyway? I fancied you could just as well make rat poison out of nicotine as anything else."

Hogston cleared his throat. "I think I can clear up that mystery, Miss Truelove. We decided to tell you all it was nicotine because we thought it would give the murderer a good scare."

Beatrice nodded. "Well, I must say I'm not sorry I did it, because it must have put the wind up Professor Bathurst good and proper. And he deserves that. But I am glad you won't hang."

"Thanks, Beatrice. That's most kind of you," Esmond sneered.

"Steady on, Professor Bathurst. We've heard enough from you today."

Wendell said, "So this brings us full circle back to the beginning, Chief Inspector. Who did it?"

Hogston nodded at Snorscomb. Snorscomb reached down and opened a briefcase. Then he pulled out a folder which he handed to Hogston.

"I have here the last will and testament of one Harold Baden Gasthorpe. It was in the boxes of papers Miss Dove and Miss Aubrey-Havelock located."

All eyes fixed on the folder as if it were a holy object.

"In his will, Gasthorpe leaves the bulk of his estate to be shared equally among any of his relatives who survive him. He specifies that this list includes all relatives, as well as cousins, but not second cousins. He does not name any relatives."

"What's the worth of his estate, Chief Inspector?" asked Devenish.

"Don't you know? Weren't you his secretary?" asked Hogston suspiciously.

Devenish took a long drag on his cigarette. "No, Chief Inspector. He always kept his financial papers locked away. I'll admit I was curious, but not curious enough to get in that kind of trouble."

"I see," said Hogston, readjusting his homburg. "The final figure is still to be determined, but his solicitors have informed us that Mr Gasthorpe's assets are in the region of £100,000. Plus his two country houses."

Devenish let out a low whistle. "Not bad. Wish I were a relative."

"That's not all," said Hogston. "The will goes on to say that if no relatives claim the estate, he leaves everything to Quenby College."

Gasp.

Dean Ossington gave out a little strangled sound. "Does that mean it all goes to Quenby?" She wrapped her necklace so tightly around her fingers that the remainder nearly choked her.

"We've checked all the birth records and so forth. We cannot find any living relatives of Mr Gasthorpe. So yes, Dean Ossington, the money goes to the college," said Hogston.

Snorscomb and Clumber began to move. To move toward Dean Ossington.

"Primrose Ossington. I am arresting you for the murder of Harold Baden Gasthorpe. You do not have to say anything unless you wish to do so, but what you say may be given in evidence."

Dean Ossington fell to the floor.

Ruby and Fina rushed to her side. "Are you all right, Dean Ossington?" asked Ruby as she lifted her head.

The dean's glassy eyes opened. "Yes, dear. Thank you," she said, slowly rising up to a sitting position. Ruby supported her back.

Snorscomb approached. He bent down and said to Fina, "Come along, Miss Aubrey-Havelock."

Fina looked up at him. She blinked. "What do you mean, 'come along', Detective Sergeant?"

The chief inspector saved him from explaining. "Miss Aubrey-Havelock. We believe you worked in collusion with Primrose Ossington. You shared the motive of wanting Gasthorpe out of the picture, as it were. I'm afraid I will be arresting you as well. You two were accomplices."

38

Clink. Clink.

The sound of keys rattled against the cell door. Fina peeled open one eye, from behind the scratchy blanket. Her mouth tasted foul. At one point during the sleepless night, she'd thought she might be hallucinating. That she wasn't locked up in a cell. But when she decided to actually pinch herself, she found it was all too real. Fina knew she suffered from mild claustrophobia but last night had brought a new meaning to the term. She'd found that if she pulled the rough blanket over her head she could trick her brain into ignoring the outside world. But she'd only discovered that trick a few hours ago.

The lock turned, the door swung open, and, for a moment, a wild hope sprang up in Fina's heart.

There was a grating sound as a metal tray slid along the floor, pushed into the room by an unseen hand. It held a greyish bun and a tin cup of water. As soon as it was fully inside, the door swung shut again with a clang.

It was all Fina could do to keep the tears from falling. She rose, clutching the blanket around herself to keep in what little warmth she had, and went to examine her breakfast. The bun was hard as stone. At that moment, she would have killed Harold Baden Gasthorpe a hundred times over, just for a cup of tea.

The memory of tea, and the thought she might not get any for a very long time, was enough to send her over the edge. Fina sat on the edge of the hard pallet they called a bed and let the tears flow down her cheeks.

~

"May I come in?" asked Ruby.

Grace nodded assent and held open the door to her college rooms. Victoria sat on a comfortable chair near the fireplace. She set down her teacup as Ruby entered the room. She gestured to the third chair, set near the table with the teapot.

"Tea, Miss Dove?" asked Victoria.

"No thank you, Professor Marlston. I will not take up much of your valuable time."

She sat down, smoothing her skirt and hair as she did so.

"Surely you haven't come to talk about my poems?" asked Grace, floating to the fireplace mantel where she kept her cigarette paraphernalia.

"No, I have some more serious business to discuss," Ruby said quietly.

Victoria rocked her head back and forth, in serious contemplation of her teacup. Without looking at Ruby, she said, "Sad, sad business about Miss Aubrey-Havelock and Dean Ossington. Who would have thought them capable of such an act?"

Ruby's right fist tightened underneath the calm exterior of her left hand. "I don't believe they did commit murder," she said, holding her head high.

"Of course you don't," said Grace sympathetically, waving

her cigarette around so that it left swirls of smoke above the fireplace. "How could you? You were so close."

"Yes, we're practically like sisters," said Ruby looking innocently from Grace to Victoria. Victoria's lips puckered. Grace let out a long stream of smoke.

"Quite," said Victoria. "Though Grace and I aren't quite like sisters ... as you know from the assault."

"Ah yes, the attack in the quad," said Ruby. "I do hope you're recovered, Professor Marlston."

"Yes, yes," she said hurriedly. "Just fine. Though I will make Bathurst pay ... one day."

"You two are good at that, aren't you?" asked Ruby.

"Good at what?" asked Grace.

"Revenge."

Victoria's eyes narrowed as she sat up straight in her chair. "What, exactly, are you here to discuss, Miss Dove?"

"I'm here to discuss how you murdered Harold Baden Gasthorpe," Ruby said simply. "And in case you get any inappropriate ideas, I have someone in the hallway watching over me."

Grace stubbed out her cigarette furiously and sat down in the chair. "What do you mean we murdered him? Why should we murder him? Because he was an odious character? If that were the criteria for murder, why, then Victoria and I would have laid our hands on half the professoriate at Oxford."

Ignoring her attempt at logic, Ruby continued. "I first saw the connection when Fina told me Grace's poems were about Liverpool. I knew Gasthorpe had grown up in Liverpool. The problem with this murder is that so many people had an opportunity to commit it, but so few really had a strong motive. So I began to think this crime had deeper roots than first appeared. The lack of documentation about extortion of particular suspects – with the exception of the will – seemed to point to some other answer.

"On a separate track, I began to wonder about the two of you. You seemed too eager for Fina and I to conclude you were lovers. Given the disastrous effects such revelations would have for the both of you, I could only conclude that something else, more scandalous, lay beneath. And then when you were attacked, Victoria, in the archway that night, Grace said something about getting revenge 'in other ways' which made me think she had already had her revenge on someone else recently."

Silence. The only noise came from an occasional spark in the fireplace.

"There was one theory which fit all the facts: you two are sisters, not lovers. And that, coupled with the fact you were both from Liverpool, as was Gasthorpe, led me to conclude you two had to be the murderers. Or at least one of you was the murderer and the other was an accomplice."

Victoria sat absolutely still. Grace, however, became animated again. "So what? You have no proof. And even if we did do it, you don't know how it was done."

Ruby smiled. "You're right. I don't have proof. I do, however, have a fairly good idea of how you did it. But that doesn't matter right now. I've come to make you a proposition."

Victoria sprang into action. "A proposition?" she said warily. "Go on."

Ruby stood up and began to pace in front of the fireplace. "You see, I think we can come to an agreement which will satisfy everyone involved – except, perhaps, the police. But I do not care about their version of what they call justice. I want Dean Ossington and Fina released from all suspicion. The scandal of this murder – which neither of them committed – would not only ruin both of them, but would take down Quenby College," she said, turning toward Victoria. "And I'm sure Professor Marlston doesn't want that."

Victoria gave Ruby an almost imperceptible nod.

"The police will go on thinking they're the perpetrators unless we have some definitive proof that someone else committed the crime. I propose the two of you write a full confession to the murder."

Grace snorted. She rose and came close to Ruby, blowing smoke in her eyes. "You bloody double-crossing scamp," she sneered. "You think you can come in here and tell us what to do?"

Ruby waved away the smoke and moved away from Grace. "I don't suppose you'd have done this without a good reason. I know you two had cause to hate Gasthorpe. What I propose is that you write the confession and in exchange you have tonight and tomorrow morning to take flight to wherever you think you might be safe. Then, late tomorrow morning, I will bring the confession to the police and they will release Dean Ossington and Fina. I know the two of you are clever enough to escape the police."

Grace and Victoria looked at each other. Ruby added hastily, "If you do not agree, I assure you I will work day and night to come up with the evidence. And you two will hang."

Victoria rose and began to move toward Ruby like a snake advancing on a rabbit.

Ruby backed up toward the window. "Remember, all I have to do is give the signal and my friend in the hallway will come running. And he has a key."

Victoria stopped halfway into her pounce and collapsed on a nearby settee. Grace collapsed next to her. They began to whisper. Ruby moved off in the direction of the door to the hallway. Just as she was nearly through the door, Grace called out to her in a shaky voice.

"We agree, Ruby. We'll sign the confession."

39

Another night in a cell. Another near-sleepless, nightmare-filled night.

"Aubrey-Havelock," intoned an official voice behind the door. The peephole cover slid open to reveal the pencil moustache of Detective Sergeant-bloody-Snorscomb.

Fina sat up, shedding her blanket onto the floor as if she were a butterfly shedding a troublesome chrysalis. She smoothed her hair.

The door opened and Snorscomb beckoned, wagging a finger at her as if she were a small dog. Fina followed dutifully. She squinted at the bright light in the hallway. He led her down one hallway, then another. Soon, they arrived at the front desk.

"Chief Inspector Hogston told me you were to wait here. Miss and Mr Dove are speaking to him and he wants you to be available," Snorscomb said to Fina, gesturing to a chair to the side of the front desk. He then turned down the hallway, leaving her with the bald desk sergeant who merely grunted at her when she took her seat.

Tick. Tick. Tick.

Fina watched the clock on the opposite wall. She listened to the patter of rain on the roof. The desk sergeant wasn't visible, except for the bald head that popped up from time to time. Occasional groans echoed from the hallway behind the desk. She shivered. The sounds must be coming from the cells.

She tried hard not to envision Ossie in the cells, like she had tried hard not to do the same with her brother. That was enough, she told herself. Time to distract. She walked over to the desk.

"Sergeant? Any chance of a cuppa? With a biscuit if you have them, please? I haven't eaten anything since eight o'clock last night."

The sergeant rubbed his cue-ball head and grumbled, "I'll see what I can do, miss." He shuffled off into what looked to be a break room. Fina stood at the desk, staring at the clutter there. Her absent stare sharpened. One of the papers had a ragged edge, as if part had been ripped away. But these weren't any old rips. Each tear had the outline of a perfect circle. James. Just like what James did to pieces of paper.

Fina's eyes widened. She looked up at the break room. She could hear a kettle boiling but there was no sign of the grumpy sergeant. She leaned over the desk, craning to get a closer view of the paper. As she did so, her eye was caught by the chief inspector's appointment diary, lying open on the desk. It was only partially visible, with half the page covered by the torn piece of paper. But she could just make out the start of a note scribbled on yesterday's entry: *4pm. J + Insp. Pic ...*

"May I help you find something, miss?" said the sergeant, proffering a cup of tea with a dry-looking biscuit.

Blast him! "I, ah, no, thank you, Sergeant," said Fina shakily. "I was trying to get a scrap of paper and a pen." She paused. "I need to write down a few things."

The sergeant complied, though he looked rather dubious.

Fina sat back down. She blew air into her biscuit, transforming its dry texture into a soft one. So James had been here – for an appointment with Hogston and another officer. What did it all mean? It seemed unlikely it was about the case. Was James the one watching them? It was hard to believe, she thought. He seemed so, well, young. But it must be an act. She sat back, feeling satisfied that for once she knew something Ruby didn't know.

A few minutes later, Fina saw a shaky but defiant Dean Ossington emerge from the back, followed by Ruby, Wendell, and Constable Clumber.

Fina jumped up and squeezed the dean as if she were as happy as a cuckoo in the nest of its neighbours. "I'm so glad to see you, Dean Ossington. Are you able to go back to college now?"

Ossie nodded as if she couldn't speak. Constable Clumber came up behind her. "I'll take you home now, madam. Come along with me. I have a car waiting in front." The odd couple padded out of the station.

Fina looked at Wendell. Wendell looked at Ruby.

"Nearly opening time. Let's go to the Peacock and Parrot. They serve an excellent lunch," said Wendell. "My treat."

"You're on," said Ruby.

Fina blinked. "You mean I can go?" Her mouth hung open. "What did you tell Hogston, you miracle worker?"

She grinned at Fina. "I promise I'll tell you all once I've started my meal."

"With a lovely pint, of course," said Fina.

"But of course."

"Could you just sign these papers, please, miss," called the sergeant, whose resentful expression suggested he did not want to hear about other people having pints.

"Happy to, Sergeant!" said Fina. She gave him a glowing smile. Suddenly he didn't seem so bad after all.

THOUGH FINA WAS NOT GENERALLY partial to steak and kidney pie, she had to admit the Peacock and Parrot did make her waver in her preferences. It was mostly that it was steaming hot, thought Fina, as she washed it down with a gulp of cider.

"Dearest, it's so good to see you out of that dreadful place," said Ruby, with a rare gush of emotion.

"It was dreadful," said Fina between forkfuls of sausage. "But I know I don't have to tell you that," she said with a sigh. "The worst part was the claustrophobia."

Ruby shivered and nodded. As if to ward off the mental picture of Fina in prison, she took a large bite of her hog roast bap. Then she looked at Wendell, busy with his fish finger sandwich. It was no small task as the fish fingers attempted to escape their fate. "I'll begin and then you can jump in when needed," she said.

Wendell gave a grateful nod as he chewed a mouthful of food.

"I'm not going to tell this story in a linear way ... because that's not really how it unfolds in my brain," said Ruby. "Let's work backwards from Dean Ossington's arrest – and from yours. She was arrested because the will said she had the most to gain from Gasthorpe's murder – and she had easy access to his pipe and tobacco all night. No one would question her comings and goings because she was the host. The police thought you two were in on it because you both had something to gain. Hogston believed you two coordinated the punch you gave Gasthorpe as a way to divert suspicion from Ossington, and perhaps get him to refill his pipe with the contaminated tobacco."

"Except that we didn't," said Fina tartly.

Ruby took a small bite of her bap, chewed and then continued. "Yes. Now do you remember the first part of the will?"

Fina nodded. "The part which says his estate goes to any surviving relatives? I must say it struck me as odd at the time. I mean, wasn't it a peculiar way to phrase a will? Wouldn't you write, 'I bequeath my hairbrush to my Great Aunt Cicely' – or something like that?"

"Yes, it struck me as peculiar as well," said Wendell. "Since I was able to see the will in advance of everyone else, I told Hogston it seemed significant. He dismissed it because he said there weren't any living relatives."

"But the fact remains he wrote it in that way for a reason," said Ruby.

"You mean he suspected he had relatives – whom he must not know about?"

"Bingo! Gasthorpe knew his father had been, well, to say 'unfaithful' would be quaint. He was a travelling salesman who seemingly spent more time selling women on his charms than on his wares. From what I can gather, Gasthorpe's mother was rolling in cash, which is most likely why Gasthorpe's father married her in the first place. Unlike the story Gasthorpe liked to tell about his hardscrabble childhood, he was born with a silver spoon in his mouth."

"So I suppose this is all leading to the fact that he had a living relative, most likely a sibling, correct?"

"Right again. Although it happened to be two siblings," said Ruby mysteriously.

Fina dropped her fork. "Bathurst? Surely not Devenish."

Wendell licked his lips and put down his napkin. "No. Grace Yingxia and Victoria Marlston."

40

"Grace and Victoria! You're pulling my leg," Fina cried. "I thought they were lovers."

Ruby wiped her hands on her napkin and pushed away her plate. "No, they're sisters. Half-sisters to each other and half-sisters to Gasthorpe. They all shared the same father."

Fina blinked.

"I already had my suspicions, but the will confirmed it," said Ruby. "It first struck me on the night when Victoria was attacked. Though it could have been from the shock, Grace acted a little oddly toward Victoria – not as someone who was overly concerned with her physical well-being. Furthermore, she said something to the effect of 'there are other ways to make him pay'. I'm not sure why, but that phrasing struck me as peculiar. It sounded like she had already thought it through. More importantly, it sounded like she had already *done so* in another case. I thought perhaps that other case might have been Gasthorpe."

"So why did you let Dean Ossington be arrested? And, more importantly, why did you allow them to arrest me?!"

"I'll return to that in a minute. Let me take you through what happened, first. Remember the first night we heard about Gasthorpe's visit?"

"You mean when Ossie, Grace and Victoria were discussing it at dinner?"

"Yes. Remember how it seemed like Ossie was the one who wanted Gasthorpe to be the guest? And Grace and Victoria were against it?"

Fina nodded.

"In fact, it was either Grace or Victoria who suggested it first. It only seemed like it was Ossie's idea. Ossie was concerned – as I found out from her later – that something might go pear-shaped with his visit and he'd stop supporting the college. Grace and Victoria manipulated Ossie by making the suggestion and then turning around and saying it wasn't a good idea. They knew her psychology well enough to know this would work. I suspect that was Victoria's idea."

"Why did they suggest it? Did they know about the will?"

Wendell said, "No, they didn't know and neither did the dean. Or I should say the dean only knew what Gasthorpe told her about the will. Grace and Victoria wanted to kill Gasthorpe for revenge, not for money."

"Revenge? For being siblings?"

"I didn't know the reason until I spoke to Grace and Victoria last night. They told me a rather tragic story about their mothers. What tied everything together for me initially in suspecting them was the connection to Liverpool. Remember when you had that conversation with Grace about Liverpool at dinner?"

"Yes. But she said her father worked on the docks and her mother worked in a newsstand. Surely Gasthorpe senior didn't work on the docks," said Fina.

"I think she told you that story to emphasise the point about her mythical dock-worker father. She knew she couldn't cover up the fact she was from Liverpool," replied Ruby. "I knew

Gasthorpe was from Liverpool as well. He'd done a good job of concealing his natural accent, but you could still hear traces of it in his speech if you knew what to listen for."

"He certainly covered it quite well. What gave him away?" asked Fina.

"Remember how he had a slight adenoidal tinge to his speech? I suspected he was covering an accent. People from Liverpool have that distinctive way of speaking. In any case, it seemed like too much of a coincidence. And then there was the odd relationship between Grace and Victoria. I thought they were lovers at first, but then something seemed, well, peculiar about their relationship."

Ruby waved away the smoke coming from Wendell's cigarette. "Grace and Victoria's mothers were destitute. Gasthorpe's father would visit them periodically and was often physically and verbally abusive. Both women witnessed this as children. He paid for Victoria's education, but not Grace's. That fit well with his son's views on women's equality for only some kinds of women," said Ruby with a sigh.

"I can see them being furious with Gasthorpe Senior, but why take it out on the son?" asked Fina.

"Because he did eventually find out about his two half-sisters. Not only did he not want to have anything to do with them, but he denied both mothers any share of his father's estate when his father died. He knew how poor and sick both of the women were, and he did nothing. Both mothers died destitute – Grace and Victoria were in their late teens when this happened."

"How did they find out about each other?"

"According to Grace, her mother knew about Victoria's mother's relationship with Gasthorpe Senior. They didn't live too far away from one another in Liverpool. Looks like Gasthorpe Senior would visit one per day."

"Makes me ill thinking about it," said Wendell.

"Yes, me too. I think Harold Gasthorpe's rise to fame and fortune, as well as his lies about his background, set the plan in motion. When I spoke to Grace and Victoria about it last night, they were still so furious, even though they had killed him. The fact he'd left them money – should they care to reveal themselves – somehow made it all worse in their minds."

"So how did they do it?"

"This case had a lot to do with eyes. The puffy, bloodshot eyes of Harold Gasthorpe right before he died. Vera's dilated eyes. My question to Grace and Victoria about spectacles."

"Yes, what was that question all about? It seemed significant, but I couldn't for the life of me figure out why," said Fina.

"I wanted to see how they reacted to a question about eyes," said Ruby.

"Now you're just teasing poor Fina," said Wendell playfully. "Spill the beans, Ruby Dove!"

"Eye-drops," said Ruby.

41

Fina felt her jaw drop.

"You mean – you mean they put nicotine in the eye-drops?"

"Yes. You see, the brilliant part of their plan was that it would be naturally assumed the nicotine came from the pipe or pipe tobacco. There wouldn't be any way to prove or disprove it. Then Wendy came up with an idea."

Wendell looked a little bashful. "Well, it was really your idea. But it did seem odd to me a murderer could plan that you would punch Gasthorpe, therefore causing the tobacco to fall out and therefore allowing Gasthorpe to top it up again with the remaining tobacco. Besides that, it had to be someone who knew at least a little about him. Grace and Victoria had interacted with him and therefore knew about the eye-drops. What's more, they knew why he took them."

"Because he had dry eyes?" said Fina doubtfully.

"It was his preferred method of taking cocaine," said Wendell. "Remember, he was the point of contact for the drug ring. Jack was wrong about him. He soon fell to taking the drug himself. Grace and Victoria both suspected the drug ring business, though they didn't understand the first thing about how it was organised. They did know, however, that he was obsessed about his eye-drop usage. They didn't know when he would use his medicine, but they were able to switch the bottle with the nicotine-filled version."

"Rather ingenious," said Fina in awe. She looked up gratefully at the plate of raspberry tart headed for their table. Fina handed Wendell a fork for him to share the tart amongst the three of them.

"Thanks, but I'm not keen on sweets," said Wendell.

"That's almost more shocking news than the eye-drops," said Fina, digging in. "But wait. I do have a question before we move on to the arrest of Ossie," she said, swallowing her first delicious bite. "This plan was awfully risky. I mean, so many things could go wrong. Victoria is obsessed with control and planning. I cannot imagine her agreeing to do this with Grace."

Ruby put down her fork. "It also stopped me from suspecting Victoria, but then I realised her increasing obsession with rules and order was a response to the strain of the murder itself. In other words, her strain made it look even more unlikely she was the murderer – a clever, unintentional trick which threw us off. As for Grace, she's the adventurous one of the pair. She has a flair for the spontaneous. The two of them together – the planner and the risk-taker – were an unstoppable combination." She paused for a sip of water. "As for your second question, I'm sure you're wondering why Wendy and I didn't say much of anything during the police theatre presentation."

"Well, yes, rather. Especially because Ossie and I had to sleep in jail," said Fina.

"I knew the police thought it was her. I also knew I had absolutely no evidence of anything, just as the police had no evidence to tie the murder to Ossington and yourself, much less directly implicate Esmond in the drug ring.

"So last night I called on Grace and Victoria. I went to

Grace's room and Victoria was there, conveniently enough for me. I gently confronted the two of them."

Fina nearly choked on her tart. "But they could have killed you!"

Wendell said, "I stood outside the door to Grace's room, listening the whole time."

"Yes, I was grateful Wendy could help out, though I honestly didn't think they'd try anything. I told them what I knew and reminded them that you and Ossington were going to hang for the murder if they didn't come forward."

"Clever – if they have a conscience," said Fina, shivering.

"I suspected they did have a conscience, and I was counting on it. I wasn't fooling myself into thinking they'd turn themselves in, because who would? But they were aware it was only a matter of time before I came up with enough evidence to turn them in. I also told them I had shared my suspicions with my brother so that if anything happened to me he would immediately go to the police."

Ruby licked her fork and set it down carefully, as if it would break the flow of her narrative if she did not. "So I made them an offer they couldn't refuse. I said if they signed a sworn statement taking responsibility for these crimes, I would give them until the next morning to escape the country. I told them I would turn in the statement to the police after that and they would have to hope they made it far enough to escape British authorities."

"So they agreed," said Fina, thoughtfully. "I wonder where they went."

Wendell replied, "That pair are clever enough. I don't think we'll see the likes of them again."

Ruby sat back, as satisfied as a cat who had polished off a bowl of cream.

"You've done it again, Ruby," said Fina. "But I do have one more question. Did Vera put the brassiere in Gasthorpe's coat?"

"That seems to be the most plausible explanation. Perhaps she thought it would confuse the police, so she slipped it in his pocket. Just in case they found she had stolen the carriage clock. Perhaps she had a half-baked idea of framing him as the thief."

Fina nodded. It seemed like a good time to surprise them both with her news. "While you two were in the back of the police station, I must admit I did a little snooping, though it was entirely unintentional."

Ruby and Wendell leaned forward.

"There was evidence James Matua had been there. Which wouldn't be so odd in itself – except that I saw a note which alluded to a meeting between Hogston, someone whose name begins with J, and another inspector. I couldn't see his whole name, but it started with 'Pic'.

Wendell let out a low whistle. "That would be Inspector Pickering. You know who he is? He's the local force connection to Scotland Yard. A liaison who often goes back and forth. I only know this because he happened to speak to Hogston while I was at the station. They introduced me to him."

"So you think James is the one who's been watching us?" said Ruby, tapping her teeth.

"Seems like the most likely explanation," said Fina. "I pondered what I knew about him. He's naïve, seemingly inept, a new student with ties to a faraway place – New Zealand."

"And he studies history, like you," said Ruby, warming to the subject. "It would be natural for you two to talk about politics and for you to gradually form a bond."

"Yes, we share anti-colonial politics, but his family is far enough away that he wouldn't really need to prove himself in any way. He probably hopes I'll spill the beans about our activities, particularly as they relate to you, Ruby."

"And I also believe he invited himself to the nightclub to watch us. Mind you, I do believe he is genuinely smitten with Gayatri – but that provided him a convenient cover to follow us," said Ruby.

Wendell nodded. "This confirms an idea which came to me when we were sitting at the police interrogation lunch," he said, pulling out a crumpled sheet of paper from his jacket pocket. Unfolding it, he said, "I realised the proverbs had something to do with the name of the person watching us ... as we discussed already. But it came to me that the proverbs themselves were anagrams. I couldn't make any full names out of the first proverb about sheep, but the second one about butchers held out two possibilities: 'Jack' or 'James Matua,'" he said in triumph. "So I surmised it was most likely to be James since the proverb included a full name anagram ... although it wasn't a perfect anagram. It was devilishly difficult because it had superfluous letters."

Ruby and Fina stared at Wendell. Fina began to clap. "That's marvellous, Wendell!"

Ruby patted her brother on his shoulder. "Excellent work, Wendy. And now that you're saying this, I remember what was bothering me. In all of our discussions of our family, Ian never once mentioned having a sister. In fact, I remember him saying once he was an only child. That must have been the signal it was that proverb told by his sister which we were to pay attention to," she said, her eyes widening.

"That's settled, then," said Wendell, leaning back in his chair and once again folding his hands behind his head.

"Assuming James was the one to search my room, however, how would he have done so without being noticed? There are strict rules about men in the women's halls," said Ruby, tapping her teeth again.

Fina replied, “He either has a co-conspirator or he dressed in feminine clothing himself to search your room.”

Ruby replied, “It seems more likely to me that he would have threatened a scout to do it. Probably Beatrice.”

“What would he have asked her to search for? Why now?”

“As for the second question,” said Wendell, “I think he used the timing of the murder investigation to his advantage. He probably thought it was his best opportunity to search – and that it would look like it was either the police or the murderer searching for something – or even the college thief.”

“What about my first question?” Fina queried.

Ruby jumped in. “I suspect he told Beatrice or some other scout to search for suspicious literature. Which could be why, of course, two of the three books stolen were Russian literature. Highly suspicious, Feens,” she said with a low, rumbling laugh.

“So if it is James, what do we do?” Fina pleaded with rising panic in her voice.

“This is the best position to be in,” said Wendell. “You know who is watching you, but they don’t know that you know. So you can handle situations to your advantage to throw them off track.”

“Yes,” agreed Ruby. “It’s much better we have the devil we know. Not that James is the devil – my guess is he naïvely thinks he’s helping himself. Or the more likely scenario is that he’s doing this because he’s been threatened in some way,” she said, looking at Wendell knowingly.

As he nodded, the smoke from his cigarette made little bumpy waves. “I’ve known a few chaps who’ve been turned because a government agent threatened their family, or threatened to expose some secret. Or even worse, they’ve been threatened with made-up charges and forced to do whatever the authorities tell them to do.”

“So you’re saying that we do nothing?” asked Fina.

"I know it seems like inactivity, but it's not. Besides, it's a much better use of our precious energy to keep an eye on him, rather than do anything. Especially when he tries to follow us," said Ruby.

"Follow us? You mean around the university?"

Ruby grinned. "That, too. But I really meant follow us in a few weeks' time. We've been invited to Italy."

"The moon runs until day catches it," said Wendell with a wink.

ENJOYED RUBY'S PORT?

I'm looking to you, dear reader, to share your views about this series. Reviews online are wonderful and word of mouth is even better.

If you enjoyed this book, I would be grateful if you spent a few minutes leaving me a review on Amazon.

The Ruby Dove Mystery Series:
The Mystery of Ruby's Sugar
The Mystery of Ruby's Port
The Mystery of Ruby's Smoke

Thank you!

BONUS MATERIAL

The Mystery of Ruby's Smoke

I would love to keep in touch with you through occasional updates (no spam) via email.

As a thank-you for signing up, I'll send you special bonus material. Join the newsletter list and download the material here.

If you've already joined my list, send me an email at rose@rosedonovan.com and I'll be sure to send it along!

ABOUT THE AUTHOR

Rose Donovan is a lifelong devotee of cozy mysteries. *The Ruby Dove Mystery Series* is her first foray into fiction, though she has written numerous non-fiction articles unraveling the mysteries of politics and injustice. Her next book in the series, *The Mystery of Ruby's Stiletto,* will be released in 2018.

Sign up to receive a thank-you and an occasional newsletter at www.rosedonovan.com.

www.rosedonovan.com
rose@rosedonovan.com

NOTE ABOUT BRITISH STYLE

Readers fluent in US English may believe words such as "fuelled", "signalled", "hiccough", "fulfil", titbit", "oesophagus", "blinkers", and "practise" are typographical errors in this text. Rest assured this is simply British spelling. *Braces* are suspenders. Electric tea kettles did exist in 1935.

There are also other formatting differences in terms of spacing and punctuation, including periods after quotation marks in certain circumstances. I certainly learned a lot when making sure the prose was accurate!

For Ben

First published in 2018 by Moon Snail Press

www.rosedonovan.com

All the characters in this book are fictitious, and any resemblance to actual persons living or dead is purely coincidental.

Moon Snail Press

Unceded Duwamish Land

Seattle, Washington

Made in the USA
Columbia, SC
22 August 2021

44147514R00143